Beyond Sunnyfields
(The Afterlife Series Book 6)
By Deb McEwan

The right of Deb McEwan to be identified as the author of this work has been asserted by her in accordance with the Copyright, Designs and Patents Act 1988.

This is a work of fiction. While some places and events are a matter of fact, the characters are the product of the author's imagination and are used in a fictitious manner. Any resemblance to actual persons, living or dead, is purely coincidental.

Cover Design by Jessica Bell

For the dead who are still with us

Author's Note

Thanks for choosing 'Beyond Sunnyfields', Book Six in my Afterlife Series. If you haven't read the first five books ('Beyond Death', 'Beyond Life', 'Beyond Destiny', 'Beyond Possession' and 'Beyond Limits') I recommend you read them before this one. Here's a summary of the story so far:

Big Ed has coerced three teenage girls into accompanying him to a party with the offer of free food and booze. They're unaware they will be groomed to have sex with older men. Melanie smells a rat, changes her mind and leaves the car before it reaches its destination.

Claire Sylvester dies in an RTA the morning after the best night of her life, along with Ron, her taxi driver. Her twin brothers Tony and Jim know she's dead before being told.

An angel named Gabriella tells Claire and Ron there's a backlog of souls waiting to be processed due to a natural disaster on earth. They're kept at Cherussola until the Committee decides their future but are allowed to visit their friends and family. Claire discovers that her fiancée had a one-night stand with her best friend and that her parents' marriage is a sham. Her father has been living a double life for many years and she has a half-sister called Melanie. She also discovers she can communicate with her brothers and that she has powers that many dead souls do not.

Ron discovers his wife had an affair with Ken, his former boss. Ken dies and goes to Hell. He is reincarnated in different forms and his soul is in constant fear and pain.

Claire's mother, Marion, and Ron's wife, Val, meet by chance and join a charity. At a get-together, Tony meets Val's daughter, Libby; they become romantically involved.

Val is already in a delicate state due to her husband's death. She is mugged (by three humans and one evil soul) during a training course and Ron begs Claire to do everything in her power to bring the muggers to justice. They discover where the muggers live and hang out, then hatch a clever plan to catch them, involving Claire's twin brothers and Jim's girlfriend, Fiona.

Melanie's friends tell her about their ordeal, so she informs the police. Big Ed and his accomplice, Sandy, kidnap her. Claire helps her brothers to find and save Melanie, but Big Ed escapes, along with Sandy. He loses his temper and kills Sandy.

Having observed Claire and Ron's work with the twins, the Committee informs Gabriella that Claire is to remain where she is for a while to help people while the angels are busy dealing with the backlog. Ron has the choice of whether to remain with Claire or to move on to eternity. Claire is sent back to Earth to visit her family and friends, not knowing whether Ron will be in Cherussola when she returns.

On her pleasant journey upwards, Sandy feels a rough jolt. The Committee have decided that she was complicit in Big Ed's crimes so must go to Hell. The decision causes a disagreement and Gabriella's brother is removed from the Committee by his mother, Amanda.

Sandy suffers torture, and humiliation in Hell but refuses to cooperate with the demons. They return her to Earth to suffer in many different guises. The Committee eventually relent and save her between reincarnations.

Unable to return to Cherussola, Claire spends time watching her family and friends. Tony and Libby marry in Gretna Green while their mothers are in Zambia, working in an orphanage for their charity. When Gabriella returns Claire to Cherussola, she introduces her to Sandy. Ron decides he wants to stay with Claire and look out for his wife Val, so delays his journey to heaven. Claire ensures that Libby knows her father watched her wedding.

Big Ed, now calling himself Gary, has fled the country and had cosmetic surgery to alter his looks. He is still supplying men with young girls but has a legitimate building business for cover. Marion and Val meet him while in Zambia. Val is instantly attracted to him, but Marion has a bad feeling – the women fall out, but Marion's instincts prove to be correct. Girls go missing from the orphanage; some presumed dead from animal attacks.

Claire meets the angel Raphael who is Gabriella's twin. The attraction is mutual.

Claire's father, Graham, overcomes his many problems and turns his life around by becoming a bodybuilder. His ex-girlfriend, Carol, softens, and they eventually get back together.

Claire has a near miss and is saved from Hell by Raphael, Gabriella and some others. Back home, Gabriella explains that Claire is being recruited to help the fight against evil. She explains how some evils are contained in a hard-to-access cave known by the locals as Hell on Earth. A number of evil souls in the guise of cockroaches are watched over by angels, disguised as bats.

Jim and Fiona marry and Tony and Libby receive a blessing at the same time.

With help from the angels and spirits, Big Ed is eventually caught and jailed for his heinous crimes. He meets an untimely death in a foreign prison and is sent to Hell.

Claire, her angel lover Raphael, and his mother try to avoid Hell's gates while fighting the demons. While they are preoccupied, serpents amass outside the cave known as Hell on Earth.

Val is depressed and struggles to come to terms with the humiliation and shame of being involved with Big Ed, who she knows as Gary. She starts to self-harm, then attempts suicide.

Gabriella mounts a rescue mission to bring back her mother, brother and Claire from the gates of Hell.

The angels are busy, and the evils take advantage. Evils are sent to the cave known as Hell on Earth in the form of serpents, to release other evil souls from their prison. While many evils are at the cave working on the escape, the angel Zach is able to escape from Hell. He meets Claire and the others involved in the rescue attempt. Claire is ordered to return to Cherussola with Zach, while Gabriella and the host attempt to rescue her mother and brother.

Harry, Big Ed's son, escapes from the cave. He needs help to avenge the wrongs against him so goes in search of his father.

After a number of reincarnations as a lap dog, the evils eventually claim Big Ed. He is taken to his rightful home in Hell. After his initiation, his masters recognise him as one of their own and realise his strength. Some try to get on his side, knowing it's only a matter of time before he becomes their superior. When he's strong enough, he punishes those who tortured him when he first arrived.

The twins are headhunted by the staff from the secret school for people with special abilities (SAP School). They are recruited and have to pretend they work for a different organisation.

Big Ed is determined to seek revenge against a number of people still living. He meets with Harry and issues orders. Harry obeys without question, knowing his son will eventually become more powerful. Until he does, Big Ed has to carry out menial tasks to learn his trade and to build his strength.

Marion dreams that Melanie is attacked. She visits Carol and they hear Melanie scream. They rush her to hospital after she is attacked by a vicious, otherworldly spider. Past events are put to bed as Marion forgives Carol and becomes close to Melanie, Claire's half-sister.

Though still in pain, Raphael notices his torture is now random. He is able to look around and realises a number of senior evils are missing. His mother transmits her thoughts, telling him it is time to escape. They do so, taking some misplaced good souls with them.

Following selection, Tony and Jim carry out various roles for the school. Their wives are suspicious, more so Fiona, who is eventually recruited.

When Marion and Libby go to collect Val from hospital, they meet her psychiatrist, Dr Basil Walters. This is life changing for Marion and the doctor.

Claire has to decide how to fight the evils, not knowing whether the other angels will return. Zach wakes up and, although he is a senior angel, it is obvious that his time in Hell has affected him. Claire notices his scars and broken body. She formulates a plan to help fight the evils and recruits Ron and Sandy. Zach is not back to full fitness and can only give limited assistance.

Raphael returns to Claire, broken. He sleeps for what seems like an eternity and she wonders if he will ever wake up.

Graham travels to weight-lifting competitions so Marion spends more time with Carol and Melanie. Val believes that Gary is visiting her dreams and Libby discovers this when she rooms with her mother during one of Mel's visits.

The Committee is too busy to hear Claire's ideas, so she decides to go ahead with her plan, without their permission.

Various attempts to discover details about the SAP School are thwarted. The twins' training is intensified as the staff want to know whether their communications with their dead sister could assist in the fight against crime.

The evils are becoming more organised and are starting to win the battle against good.

After a period of peace, Val's nightmares return and become worse. She knows that Gary is in her head when she's asleep. As well as being terrified, it's driving her insane.

Marion has a secret relationship with Basil, not yet ready to tell her family about him. While she's away, Melanie has nightmares involving Big Ed.

Big Ed practises his possession techniques. Once he's satisfied he can overcome any hosts, he sets out to find an evil person who he can bring into line.

Claire has a run-in with an evil known as Goth, who later escapes. When they next meet, she transforms Goth's body into a cockroach. Goth has arranged a surprise for Claire's brothers, so Claire has to leave her before being able to transform her head.

Big Ed possesses mad Martin, the country's most notorious serial killer, during a prison transfer. He escapes and commits further murders. Eventually, Big Ed dominates him, and he is forced to go along with his plans. Big Ed, now in the body of Mad Martin goes to claim Val.

Gabriella and Amanda return to work and Claire is promoted to angel while on a mission. With Gabriella's help, they find Goth-Roach, turn her head into a roach, and deliver her to the cave.

Claire sleeps on return to Cherussola and is awoken by Raphael. He is scarred and damaged but is going to get better.

Claire, Gabriella, Raphael, Zach and Ron watch as Mad Martin heads for Marion's apartment, buoyed on by the voice in his head. Val is home alone as he enters the house and makes his way to her bedroom. When he speaks, Val knows that Gary has taken over his mind and body. He walks toward her carrying a knife and she backs towards the window. Opening it, she climbs out onto the ledge. He joins her and Val embraces him, then jumps. Libby and Tony pull up in their car in time for Libby to see her mother and the man landing on the concrete.

As Claire is transforming Big Ed, a dark invisible presence arrives and drags him and Mad Martin away. The Devil doesn't show himself but torments the souls until they can take no more. He then shows himself and destroys them permanently. When he'd finished with them, the Devil turns to Claire and undresses her with his eyes, before putting a hand on her shoulder and pushing her downwards. He starts to torture her as he pushes her further down towards his home. As she loses hope, Claire hears the voice of the Lord. She feels warmth on her body and the Devil's mark disappears from her shoulder.

The Lord and Devil fight until the Devil returns to Hell with his tail between his legs, vowing to win the next round.

When trying to give the recently deceased Val a second chance at life, an angel makes a mistake causing the soul of a child to be suspended in the ether where she floats aimlessly, believing she's dreaming.

A natural disaster causes a fissure in the cave known as hell on earth. By the time the guards realise what's happened, it's too late to recapture the evil souls who have escaped. Two escapees, Goth-Roach and Harry, are the former enemies of Claire and her family. They find the young child's soul and are determined to groom her, so she can carry out the devil's work.

While Claire's twin brothers, Tony and Jim, are learning to enhance their telepathic abilities at the

SAP School, Libby, Tony's wife, is unable to come to terms with the death of her mother and seeks solace elsewhere. She meets Cassie, who murders her – Libby is eventually reincarnated, and Cassie is punished for her crimes.

The Devil's servants torment dead souls by returning them to earth in various guises. They also arrange for a number of children to be possessed so they can carry out evil deeds. Chaos ensues as stories of children committing heinous crimes grab the media's attention. The twins attempt to contact their dead sister, Claire, for help, but she doesn't respond.

Souls are stolen from both sides as the battle between good and evil persists.

Goth-Roach has ambitious plans to exact revenge on Claire by destroying the angel and her family, and to increase her standing with the Devil, but her plan doesn't work. She's transformed and banished to the cave.

Ron and Sandy are eventually reunited, in a good place. Claire's mum saves the life of Mel (Claire's half-sister) and marries Basil.

All hell is let loose in a small Dutch town when an evil spirit inflicts terror on an orphan who grows into a troublesome youth. The evil spirit later possesses her and as she grows into a beautiful woman, it's harder to repel the spirit.

Tony meets the beautiful woman by chance and ignores his dead sister's advice. This comes back to haunt him later on.

The angel Claire is tested by the ultimate committee. The temptation is so great that she risks failure and separation from Raphael. She has to decide whether to pass the tests or risk the wrath of the committee by looking after those she loves.

The Director discovers someone is trying to expose the secret facility. Investigations by the twins show that four people want to destroy the headquarters/school. The organisation fails to save it.

Marion risks her own life to save a baby when the school is set on fire. They later discover that the baby is Tony's child. A very special child indeed.

And now book six...

Chapter 1 – Dee Benson

Staff Sergeant Dee Benson survived the blast without injury. She was the only one who did.

Dressed in combats, she was now standing outside the office of her commanding officer, waiting to be called in for him to pick through her report of the incident, she assumed.

The door opened and Lieutenant Colonel Watts nodded at her. 'Come in Staff.' Dee saluted and followed him into the office. 'Remove your head dress and take a seat.'

She did as ordered and waited while he shuffled some papers. Seconds later there was a knock on the door and a lance corporal, who Dee didn't know, entered, carrying a tray containing two mugs. *So it's not an interview without coffee*, Dee thought as the CO thanked the soldier and waited for him to leave the office.

'Today I want to talk to you about some of the missions you've been involved in, Staff, as well as your future, and another role for which you've been specially selected.' They both laughed wryly at the last, knowing that *specially selected* usually meant that nobody else was available for, or wanted, the job.

'Firstly, can you explain to me in your own words how you managed to get off the boat before the missile hit?'

'Have you read my report, Sir?'

The CO picked up some papers from his desk. 'Yes, I have it here in front of me, but I want to hear it in your own words.'

Dee looked down, knowing that she would struggle to believe what had happened if someone else told her, but it was the truth and she now looked her CO in the eyes as she started to talk. 'We'd recce'd the area and hadn't met any tangos. We were leaving on the Rigid Raider when we heard the helicopter. It all happened so quickly, but Mark, sorry, Sir, Colour Sergeant Murphy, shouted, '*Incoming*', and the next thing I know I was thrown from the boat and landed in the water.'

'From the force of the blast?'

Dee sighed. 'You have my report, Sir, and you will see that it says before the blast, not after. An invisible force threw me from the boat before the missile hit. I know it sounds ludicrous but that's what happened.'

'And you're sure about that?'

'Absolutely one hundred per cent certain, Sir.'

'And who or what was this invisible force?'

'No idea, Sir.' She'd become so used to that answer that she almost believed it herself.

'I see. I have some other reports in front of me. One from Afghanistan when you escaped injury when other members of your team were injured; another on exercise when you were thrown from a truck before it crashed; and in the crew room when you couldn't move from a chair to make a brew and your colleague who did so received an electric shock from an unsafe kettle. Are these about right?'

'Yes, Sir. And all unexplainable as you know.' The information was well documented, and Dee had undergone additional psychiatric evaluation, even though there had been witnesses to each *unusual* event.

'I wanted to ensure that you still stand by everything you say, Staff.'

'I do, Sir, and I also realise that my future in this unit is untenable. It was funny first of all when the team nicknamed me Lucky, but now it's wearing a bit thin. And if I ask for leave or am unable to do something for whatever reason, the others are now suspicious and wonder if something's going to happen to them. I've made them quite superstitious, although it's not my fault, and they seem to think there's some sort of divine intervention going on.'

'And what if there is?'

'I don't know what's going on, Sir. Only that I can't explain it–I've come to a decision.'

'Which is?'

'I'm leaving the Army. I can't do what I want any more so I'm getting out and I'm going to look for another career.'

'Well, this brings me to what I mentioned earlier. You have been specially selected for something, but I'm afraid I can't tell you what it is.'

'But if I don't know, how can I make the decision of whether I want to do it?'

'I can't tell you, Staff, but others can. It's all very cloak and dagger and, try as I might, I've been unable to obtain any further information.'

Dee pondered this for a moment. If the CO of the Special Operations Unit didn't know what the job or role was, it must be top secret, or even higher. She decided to do some digging and contact some of her Intelligence Corps mates.

'And it's no good contacting your Int. Corps family,' he said, seemingly reading her thoughts. 'I've already tried that without any luck. All I can tell you is that you'll have two weeks leave, then report to the training centre at Brecon where you'll be given further instructions.'

'I'm not sure, Sir. I came in here intent on handing in my notice, but now…'

'Well, Staff, why don't you think about things while you're on leave, and if this has piqued your

3

interest, report to Brecon after your leave and see what it's about? If you're still intent on leaving after that, you can apply to be discharged then.'

She couldn't deny that she was curious, and the CO had probably counted on that.

'Well?'

'Yes, Sir. That's what I'll do.'

'Good, good,' he said, before getting up from his desk and walking around to the other side. 'I think that's the right decision. I hope to hear good things about you in the future, Staff. Good luck and thanks for everything you've done for us here.'

He held out his hand and she shook it, then put her beret back on and saluted. 'Thanks, Sir,' Dee said, and turned about smartly and walked quietly out of the office.

Two hours later she was dressed in jeans, t-shirt and bomber jacket as she entered the Queen Victoria Hospital and headed for the military wing.

Her ex, Colour Sergeant Mark Murphy, was sleeping, and she studied the handsome, muscular man as she took a seat next to his bed. He was strong and determined and she knew that the loss of his right leg from the knee down wouldn't dampen his enthusiasm for life. He opened his right eye first, followed by his left, then smiled.

'I should be so lucky, lucky, lucky, lucky...' Mark sang the lyrics from the Kylie Minogue song.

'Shut up,' Dee said, then thumped him none-too-gently on his upper arm.

'Oi! I am injured you know.'

'Well you haven't lost your sense of humour, I see.'

'No, just half a leg. And they told me yesterday it wouldn't grow back either. Gutted!'

They both laughed at the gallows humour for a moment, then Mark became serious. 'I might not have to leave the service, but this is life-changing. Not sure I want to be a desk-jockey.'

'It's early days yet, Mark. You need to give it time before you decide the best course of action and what's right for you.'

'You're right. And at least we're still here. Not like poor Smudge. When's his funeral?'

'Next week.'

They talked about the funeral and Mark's treatment before he raised the subject of the attack. 'I saw what happened, Dee. What did it feel like?'

It was no good denying it as she had to some of the others, as he knew when she was lying. But she wasn't going to tell him her theory on who she thought was looking out for her, or anyone else for that matter. Nobody knew that. 'As far as I can remember, it was like an invisible force lifted me off the boat and into the sea.'

'Scary?'

'That's the thing, it wasn't scary. Every time something weird like this has happened to save my life, it's never frightened me. It's like I know who, or whatever it is, is trying to stop me from being hurt.'

'It is weird though.'

'Understatement. Anyway, I can't work in the Section anymore, not when this keeps happening. It's making people superstitious. The boss more or less told me earlier today, so I'm off to pastures new.'

'But it'll be fine and…'

'It won't, Mark. I've been thinking about it for a while now and this last job,' she pointed to his leg, 'it's made up my mind. I'm off.'

'So, what's the plan?'

'Don't know yet. I'll take some leave and then make my mind up.' Dee didn't realise until now that she didn't want to share the information her boss had given her.

5

'Why don't we get back together and give it another shot?'

She laughed. 'How many times do I have to tell you that's not going to happen?'

'I won't cheat again, I promise.'

'You said that after the first time, Mark, and I was stupid enough to believe you. It's almost like you can't help yourself. You see a pretty girl or someone you think is a challenge and use that to think,' she pointed to his groin, 'instead of your brain.'

'But I...'

'No way. I shouldn't have given you a second chance and there's no way you're having a third!'

They chatted about other things for a while before Dee got up to leave. 'Shall I pick you up for the funeral?'

'Yeah, and I guess that'll be goodbye to you, Dee, as well as Smudge?'

She nodded, then kissed him on the cheek and left the ward.

Dee picked up a Chinese takeaway on the way home and ate it in front of the TV in the apartment she rented, accompanied by a few glasses of dry white wine. Mess life was okay, and the camaraderie was great, but aside from duty personnel, it was dead at weekends. *I'm so rock and roll*, she thought as she wondered what other members of the section were doing on their Saturday night. Then she thought of her best friends. To be fair, Trish and Sue had both called for a catch up, and both had asked when they could visit – Trish from her home in Germany, and Sue, from hers in Scotland. Nothing firm had been arranged but they'd all agreed to see each other again, soon.

A bottle and a half of wine later, Dee's foggy brain told her she might now be able to sleep without the dreams–it lied.

6

Her dream took her back to the blast on the boat. She was watching from the sea as the other members of her team were all thrown into the air. This time, she watched as different parts of their bodies landed next to her in the sea, a bit at a time, and none survived. Dee cried out in her sleep, but the nightmare didn't wake her. It ended as quickly as it had started, and still sleeping Dee's dream allowed her to feel her mother's soothing hand stroking her hair. 'Don't worry, my baby girl, Mummy and Daddy love you, and so does Trevor. Everything's going to be all right.'

Dee sighed in her sleep and her breathing settled. The rest of her night passed peacefully.

The following morning, she took the wine bottles out of the fridge and emptied them down the sink. Knowing she would need to be mentally and physically fit if she was going to accept the challenge in Brecon, she decided to use her leave period to eat well and hone both her physical and mental skills by pushing herself to the limit.

Dee started her days with a session of Asana Yoga, before training her brain to sharpen her reaction times; she was right-handed and practised using her left hand to brush her teeth, make a brew or open and close doors, hoping that this would improve her cognitive skills. After a hard gym session, she often played video games in order to help her speed up her reaction times – this was much more fun than using her non-dominant hand for mundane tasks.

By the time she reported to Brecon for duty, Dee believed she was ready for anything the Army wanted to throw at her.

She had no idea that her next assignment would have nothing to do with the Army.

Chapter 2 - Trevor

Trevor watched one of his charges knowing he could do nothing to save him from himself.

Ruben Groot was still haunted by the decision he'd made to help discredit Bishop Lange when he was a teenager. He sat in a chair in his flat with a half empty whisky bottle in front of him and picked up the bottle of tablets. He gave them a shake, then threw them across the room, where they hit the wall and fell, safety cap unopened, onto the floor. A day didn't pass when he didn't curse the day he'd been weak enough to go along with Christina's plan, all of those years before. If only he'd had the guts to stand up to the evil bitch! Therapy, anti-depressants and his success as a Youth Worker had done nothing to lessen this guilt. Tears ran silently down his cheeks as he got up and walked into his bedroom. Sitting down, he looked into the mirror, staring at his reflection and wondering for the millionth time why he had been so weak.

Ruben had no idea who Trevor was, or that he was in the room, crying with him. His guardian angel had tried to protect him but now knew there was nothing he could do to lessen Ruben's pain, and he waited for it to get worse before getting better.

Ruben picked up the pistol he'd left on his bedside table and pointed the barrel at the side of his head. He took his final breath before squeezing the trigger.

Trevor wiped his eyes and, now the deed was done, prepared to welcome the tortured soul. A new host had already been identified and Ruben was to have another chance at life before his final destination in eternity was decided.

After delivering Ruben, Trevor was told to report to the angel Gabriella. He was intrigued and could hardly contain his excitement. It was his first time he was to have an audience with a member of the committee, and such an important one at that. He knew it would either be very good or very bad news. He tried not to be greedy and self-important, but secretly hoped his hard work was to be paid off with a promotion.

It wasn't the news Trevor had hoped for.

'You have to stop interfering in your sister's life if you want to progress as an angel,' Gabriella said to the teenager. 'I know it's hard but…'

'She has nobody, and if I don't…'

'It's got to stop, Trevor, or there will be consequences.'

'Such as?'

Gabriella was beginning to feel like a headmistress telling off a naughty boy. She tried to be compassionate and understanding but Trevor had the ability to try her patience to the limit. 'Such as periods of constant supervision where you won't be allowed to visit or watch over her. Or even another stint in the bat cave.'

'I see. Can I go now?'

'Yes, you can go.'

As he left, Gabriella hoped that this time he'd taken her orders on board and would do as she said. Deep down, she felt his behaviour wouldn't change, and the Committee Chair was at a loss as to what to do for the best. Like Claire, he was a maverick, but he was also loyal and hard-working and she didn't want to take him away from his other duties, which were considerable. He was also fun to be around, very good for morale when anything went wrong, and was great at winding-up any evils he encountered.

Weighing up the pros and cons, she decided to give him this final chance and see how it worked out.

Chapter 3 – Sunnyfields Opens

'I now declare Sunnyfields open!' Sir Paul Field said, as he cut the ribbon to his flagship store on London's Oxford Street. His glamorous wife, affectionately referred to by the public as Lady Stacey, smiled along with her husband until she saw the staff struggling to hold back the hordes of shoppers. Her husband grabbed her arm and pulled her into the cordoned off area pretty sharpish as the crowd of shoppers rushed inside, as if escaping from a war zone rather than seeking out bargains in the new, swanky store.

As the buying frenzy went on below them, only an elite group knew the purpose of most of the top floor.

The Director looked out of his window, down at the queue of people waiting to get in, crowding the pavements and spilling out onto the road. He was determined that the secret of his operations centre at Sunnyfields would stay that way, and hoped that his plan to hide in plain sight would work.

The traffic was always heavy in London, despite the congestion charge, so the staff at the operations centre tended to arrive by public transport where possible and exited the underground from Bond Street Station. It took less than two minutes to walk the eight hundred or so feet to arrive at the department store. Jim and Tony were no exception and had received their briefing about how to access their offices.

Like members of the public, most of the time they entered the store through the main entrance at the front, but unlike those who were there purely to pick up a bargain or an extravagance, they then took the stairs down to the underground carpark which was a level below the main delivery area that most shoppers were unaware of. The car park and delivery area had been built at the junction between Oxford Street and

Orchard Street. There were no signs to indicate this car park existed. It was split into two floors with spaces for chief executives of the company and the second section above was separated with a loading and unloading bay for delivery vehicles. The majority of deliveries from other suppliers went directly to the company's main warehouse in Nottingham; those direct to store were carried out by Sunnyfields logistics department during the quieter hours of the night. The exception was for perishable items where deliveries from outside suppliers were arranged on a strict basis with drivers given a booking reference number and a specific arrival time. Even with the unpredictability of the London traffic, there was only a thirty-minute leeway permitted, either side of the arrival time. In addition, drivers were not allowed to leave their vehicles, and no toilet or canteen facilities were provided for them. A Dock Marshal was employed to control the flow of vehicles, and to allocate loading bays where required, and woe betide any driver who didn't adhere to the instructions or directions from the Dock Marshal. As with most new setups, the company knew it would take a few weeks for word to get around amongst the driver community that they had to follow strict instructions, or risk their company losing business with Sunnyfields, or even their own jobs.

Fortunately for the operations staff, the private car park section was on a lower level and couldn't be seen by the delivery vehicle drivers, or the staff managing the commercial deliveries. This wasn't by accident.

As Jim and Tony arrived at the private parking level, Jim pushed open the door marked *Staff Only*. Had a lost member of the public entered, they would have found themselves in a small room where some boxes were stacked against the wall on the other side, and might have assumed there was nowhere else to go.

They wouldn't have noticed that a camera was hidden amongst the lights in the ceiling.

The twins walked to the other side of the room and Jim pressed his index finger on the wall at his eye level, as he'd been instructed. The system recognised his fingerprint. There was a soft buzzing sound and the wall slid open. They walked through and the panel closed behind them. The area they found themselves in looked like a foyer of a small hotel with a reception desk. They smiled when they saw who was on duty. 'Hi, Mac. You decided to relocate then?'

The security guard smiled back. 'Tony and Jim. Good to see you, fellas.' He was one of a small number of people who didn't get the twins mixed up and looked at them in turn when he said their names. 'I fancied a change of scenery and the offer was too good to refuse. Three weeks on, one week off, so I can return to the Highlands every month and tell Norma all about these softie southerners.'

They all chuckled as the twins carried on past Mac to the lift area. They called the lift, entered, and waited for the door to close. There were only two buttons they could choose to press; a big red *'Press in an emergency'* button and an *'Open/Close'* one. The lift only stopped on two floors – where they already were and the top floor of the building, or the Operations Centre for the organisation, which was formerly known as SAP, Special Ability People. Since closing their school and Operations Centre in the Scottish Highlands, the organisation had split into two distinct areas with two completely different purposes.

The Operations Centre at Sunnyfields – now simply referred to as Sunny – was the home base for those trainees; the *Special People* and those without paranormal abilities – who had completed training and honed their unique skills. The British Army's training centre in Brecon was used to select and train recruits.

12

The recruits who would be used in the field were required to carry out basic agent training in order to accompany qualified personnel on a low-level mission. The mission was a pass or fail test, and at this stage, recruits thought they were joining a new branch of the British Army and were unaware of the secret organisation and its purpose. Those who passed were trained further in field craft. This consisted of soldier training, followed by some advanced aspects of training used by the special forces. If they were deemed to be talented enough to work as a field agent, they then had to undergo a two-year apprenticeship before being considered for their own missions. The vetting process was stringent, and personnel were rejected if they had any criminal records aside from for driving offences, or minor misdemeanours occurring as a result of immaturity. They could also be rejected if their family backgrounds couldn't be checked thoroughly, or if any inconsistencies or flaws were found when checking out their close relatives. These could be related to criminal activity, addiction, dishonesty, or anything else that the Director or his senior staff deemed to be suspect. If any of the staff had a gut instinct that something wasn't quite right about a trainee, that could also be grounds for rejection, or further investigation at the very least.

Those with special abilities who did not have the competence, talent, skills, or desire to become field agents were trained in Brecon, but in a different section. Their training included administration, engineering, IT technology, communications and the individual training that their particular ability required. All recruits were required to undergo psychiatric evaluation. When fully qualified, these personnel would mostly be employed at the operations HQ in Sunnyfields and would not be sent on field missions.

The high dropout rate was testament to how tough the training was, and some recruits realised they had chosen the wrong career. Without exception, these were the people with less natural talent and ability. Some sidestepped to the military, and the Army's Intelligence Corps often recruited these individuals. Having signed the Official Secrets Act, those discharged from the school knew they were not permitted to discuss any aspect of their training with anyone outside the organisation. Unfortunately, this didn't stop the occasional failed recruit from doing so, but, to date, nobody who had been discharged had known enough to make a difference and those who did talk were rarely believed by their friends. Even so, there was a small section at Sunny that was required to monitor the movements and conversations of former recruits and any misdemeanours were dealt with silently and swiftly, with no cases of repeat offenders.

After settling into their new offices and carrying out some routine surveillance for the Director during their first few weeks down south, Tony received a call from Marion who had some worrying news.

Chapter 4 – In the Suburbs

Since her attempted murder in the former headquarters and training centre that had burned down in Scotland, and during her recovery, Marion had taken a leave of absence from the company. They'd left the door open for her to return but she couldn't see it happening. She was content to stay at home, and to bring Eva and Spike to her and Basil's home while Tony went off to work. Basil was happy with this arrangement and they'd converted a bedroom into a nursery for Eva. The families lived on two estates and were all within a short walking distance of each other.

It was the Thursday prior to the Bank Holiday weekend and both Basil and the twins had the weekend off. They were all going to get together at Jim and Fiona's for a barbecue on Saturday evening, weather permitting.

As long as Spike was with her, Marion was happy to leave Eva sleeping. Her granddaughter and four-legged protector didn't stir as Marion picked up her phone to call Fiona.

'Do you want to give me the shopping list and I'll pick up the ingredients for Saturday today? Save you a job tomorrow?'

'You're up early, Marion, and well organised. Another dream?' Fiona said, ignoring her mother-in-law's question due to concern about her mental well-being.

'Basil said it's quite normal to have dreams and even flashbacks for some time after a traumatic event. I don't have flashbacks and I'm fine. But thanks for asking.'

'It's only because we're worried and…'

'I appreciate that, Fiona, but as I said, I'm fine. I know you have a busy job so don't want to take up any more of your time. Shall we go through the shopping list?'

Knowing it was pointless trying to discuss the matter further, Fiona backed down, and a few minutes later Marion had a list of enough food to feed a small army.

'I'll drop it off at yours later and see you on Saturday.'

After they said goodbye, Marion had no idea that her shopping trip would be scuppered by forces beyond her control.

*****

Tony's large German Shepherd, Spike, sat up as a presence in the bedroom woke him. He watched the two, dark ball shapes hovering above Eva as she started to toss and turn, and he growled menacingly. Although it wasn't loud, Marion was tuned into her granddaughter and her son's dog. She put down her coffee and started up the stairs.

The shapes changed into something similar to human forms. One was what would have been considered traditionally good-looking until you looked into his eyes. They were dark brown and held within them memories of the unspeakable cruelty they'd inflicted on small children, animals, and any adults, as the fancy took him. He had more fun with the vulnerable so preferred children and animals. The face smiled as it looked down at Eva.

'Jolly good,' he said, rubbing his hands together. 'I like them young.'

The accomplice, who looked like a monster from a horror movie, cackled. Eva cried out in her sleep and Spike barked.

When she entered the bedroom, Marion couldn't see anything amiss. But she felt the atmosphere. She couldn't see or communicate with the dead but the same feeling she had had on the day the

16

mad woman had tried to kill her, when she had saved her granddaughter's life, swept over her. As terrifying as that time had been, the overriding memory of that day had been the pure, unadulterated joy of discovering she had a granddaughter, then seeing her beloved, deceased daughter Claire, and having a conversation with her. Doctors had since said that her brain had been playing tricks on her, but Marion was convinced it had been real. Although Basil was sceptical and insisted it was her brain attempting to show her what she wanted to see during her death experience, he no longer pushed the point. Interestingly, every time she now raised the subject, Basil and the twins remained neutral, commenting that as long as she was happy that was all that mattered, before moving swiftly on to other subjects.

Even though she was convinced that Claire would eventually intervene, it did nothing to stop Marion's dread at feeling an evil, unworldly presence in the room. She knew it was out to get her granddaughter whose extraordinary abilities were as yet unknown to all of her loved ones.

Eva's face was screwed up and Spike had stopped barking now he'd alerted Marion to the problem, but his eyes were following something that she couldn't see. He snarled at whatever it was, baring his teeth in warning.

'I've told you before to leave us alone,' Marion told the intruders matter-of-factly as she looked to where Spike's eyes were looking. 'My daughter is an angel and she'll sort you out, no bother.'

The atmosphere changed.

Seeing the angels approach, the evils knew it was time to leave.

'Another time. We've plenty of surprises in store for you, goody two shoes,' said the one with the cruel, dark eyes.

Marion watched as the tension in Spike's body disappeared. She couldn't see the man with wings who had appeared above the cot or the demons Spike had growled at turning back into dark orbs, then disappearing, tout suite.

Spike thumped his tail on the floor as a woman he'd seen before also appeared above Eva.

She said, 'Good boy, Spike,' and he knew his charge was no longer in danger.

Having heard the warning from the evil beings, Claire frowned, but she knew lots of them were full of bluff and bluster, so decided to ignore it. 'Well done, Mum,' she said, even though she knew her mother couldn't hear her.

Eva, now six months old, opened her eyes.

'Hello, beautiful,' Claire said to her and the baby gurgled, then smiled up at her Auntie. 'We have work to do but will come back and check on you later.'

Both Claire and Raphael gave Eva a little wave before disappearing.

Now, feeling they were alone in the bedroom, Marion smiled. 'Up and out early today,' she said, as she first opened the curtains then lifted Eva out of her cot. 'A quick walk for you, Spikey, then Eva and I are off to the shops and you can keep the nasties out of the house while we're out.'

Spike thumped his tail and Eva made gurgling noises in response to her Nanna's chatting.

Ninety minutes later, Marion entered the supermarket with Eva dangling in a pouch from her chest. She grabbed a trolley and started checking her list, chatting to Eva as she did so.

'We're going to need washing powder, then we'll get some of that coffee your daddy likes, before going to the meat counter to get the stuff for Saturday.'

As she was looking for Tony's special coffee, Marion noticed four floor staff and a man in a suit heading to the other side of the aisle to where she was shopping. She continued browsing but couldn't help overhearing their conversation.

'There's millions of them, Marty, giant ants all over the shelves and they're climbing…'

'It's Mr Phillips at work, Cathy, I've already warned you about this–and I think you'll find the proper term is an army of ants. It might look like there's millions, but I'm sure there's just a few–Oh, My, God!'

'See, I told you…'

Marion was curious to see what was going on. About to walk around to the other side of the aisle she felt a warning shiver run up her spine and the hairs on her neck stood on end. 'Oh no!' she said, as something made her look up.

An invisible force picked Marion up and moved her further along the aisle. Seconds later, the sound of glass shattering could be heard throughout the supermarket, as jars from the top shelf crashed to the floor where Marion had been standing seconds earlier, and also into the trolley containing her shopping.

Eva started to cry, and Marion put her arms around her, trying her best to soothe her granddaughter.

'Your Auntie Claire saved us again, Eva,' she said, feeling anything but calm. She looked upwards towards the shelf that now lay empty. 'You can't get us!' she said, in an attempt to convince herself as well as the evil presence. 'Whatever you try, my daughter will always be with us to save us from harm. Now leave us alone!'

The dark-eyed demon chuckled. 'Next time,' he said, before disappearing, and leaving his posse of insect underlings to their fate.

'Are you all right, Madam?' Even though she was still upset, Marion recognised the voice of the man the woman had called Marty. She turned to look at him. His face was ashen, and he looked more shocked than she felt.

'We're fine, thank you. It seems we had a lucky escape. What happened?' she asked.

'Nothing like this has ever happened before. It appears that, er, the coffee jars may have been stacked incorrectly and fell over. I'll have to speak to the health and safety department and write a report. I can only apologise…'

'What about the ants?'

Marion wouldn't have thought it possible, but even more colour drained from his face.

'Yes, ants. I heard one of your staff… Oh never mind. Let's take a look.'

'I'm not sure that's a good idea…'

Marion ignored him and, the adrenaline still flowing after being saved from a nasty attack, walked around the aisle to the other side. Her eyes followed a huge trail of ants heading from the floor to the top shelf and back down again. It was like a freak of nature; the width of the trail was at least as tall as she was, and she realised that the sheer force of these insects had pushed the jars off the shelf. This was more than a freak of nature. *I was right, and they've definitely come to get us*, she thought, as she took an involuntary step backwards, feeling her legs weaken.

'I've got you,' the shop manager said, as he put a firm arm around her to stop her from falling over. 'Let's get you and the baby away from this and we'll go and sit down.'

Marion hardly noticed the area being taped up and the other shoppers being chivvied out as they made their way to the front of the shop. On the other sides of the checkouts, one of the shop assistants brought her a chair and Marion sat down. Now over the initial shock of what had happened and feeling less wobbly, she tried to process the thoughts running through her mind and knew if she shared them with the supermarket manager who was now standing in front of her, he would think she was bonkers.

Eva had calmed and was back to her happy self and Marion looked through the windows where shoppers were gawping, trying to discover why they weren't allowed inside. The manager's eyes followed hers as they watched the shoppers being moved to one side as a large white van with the words, *Pest O Kill*, written on the side in red letters, next to a dead ant logo, parked up. Men, dressed in what looked like white versions of the Ghostbusters uniforms, complete with packs on their backs, jumped out and headed for the door. A police car arrived shortly after.

'Shall we go to my office?' the manager asked, as Marion stood up.

'Actually, I just want to get my granddaughter home.'

'But I need to take a statement from you, and the police may want…'

'That's fine. I can leave you my telephone number and the police can phone me if they want a statement.'

'You've had a terrible shock, Mrs…?'

'Call me Marion.'

'You may need a doctor to check you're both okay, Marion. Just in case. The shock you know?'

'We're fine, thank you. And the best thing for both of us is to get home, although I do still need to do my shopping.'

'We'll arrange that for you, don't you worry,' Mr Phillips said. 'Do you have a list?'

Marion handed him her shopping list, and they exchanged phone numbers.

'Now, do you need a lift? I can arrange that too if you wish? Would you like a cup of sweet tea first, before you go?'

'It was a shock, but I feel fine now, honestly. And I'm all right to drive my own car home.' But as she stood, Marion's legs felt wobbly again and she sat back down quickly. A policewoman entered the store and approached them both. Mr Phillips nodded to an assistant and had a quick word. The assistant smiled at Marion as he walked away and had a chat with the policewoman out of her earshot.

A few minutes later, Marion agreed to let the policewoman drive her home in her own car, and for her short statement to be taken there. One of the policewoman's colleagues would be along to pick her up later. She left the supermarket with the firm assurance that her shopping would arrive later that day.

'I'm so sorry for what's happened here today, Marion. And I hope it won't put you off from...'

'Don't worry, Mr Phillips. This event was out of your control, or anyone else's for that matter.'

'Well, that's very kind of you to say so and along with our health and safety department, I will do my utmost to ensure...'

Marion headed to the door, with a quick, 'Goodbye,' as he carried on talking.

After being welcomed home by Spike, she settled Eva and put the kettle on. While she was getting the tea things ready in the kitchen, Marion made a quick call to Tony.

'When we were shopping...' She told Tony that an incident had happened and that she would explain later, when the policewoman had left. He listened intently.

'Is Eva okay, Mum? And how are you? I'll be home as soon as I can.'

'We're fine and are home now. I'm about to give a statement to the policewoman who drove us home. The press were already gathering at the supermarket when we left.'

'Okay. I'll be on my way shortly.'

Marion took the tea through and gave the policewoman her statement as quickly as she could.

'So you heard the staff talking and the next thing was a crash with the broken jars just missing you? Is that right?'

'That's what happened, yes. It was a close call and really frightened my granddaughter.' She nodded to Eva who was on the floor playing with a toy and being watched very carefully by Spike.'

'The manager said somebody saw you being lifted from danger.'

'Oh really? There was nobody else in the aisle and I'm sure I would have remembered if that happened.' She shook her head and frowned, doing a good impression of being exasperated and hoping she'd given Tony enough information for the company to send someone to the supermarket to wipe the CCTV footage of the event.

When she was satisfied that she had all the information she needed, the policewoman called for a lift back to the station. They chatted about Eva while she waited for her transport, and Marion tried to hide her impatience.

She needed to arrange a meeting with Basil, Tony, Jim and Fiona, Violet and, most importantly, the Director, as soon as possible.

*****

Knowing Tony would be on the train and unable to talk in private, Marion called the office. The Director and staff were in a meeting and someone who Marion didn't know answered the phone. The woman sounded pleasant enough until she informed her that she'd made an appointment for Marion to come in to see the Director.

'No, I can't and won't come into the office next week!' Marion responded. 'This is a matter of life and death so please go and interrupt the meeting and get someone to call me as soon as they can.'

It was Tony who called back some five minutes later. The shopping had arrived and she'd just finished putting the perishable goods in the fridge before he called. 'I need to speak to you two, Basil and Fiona and the Director and Violet and I...'

'Okay, Mum, we'll do it by video conference...'

'Tony!' The severity of her tone made him stop mid-sentence and he felt like he had when he'd been caught doing something naughty as a young lad.

'The meeting will be this Saturday, and if necessary, it can take place at Jim and Fiona's either at the barbecue or before. Think of this as the most important mission you will ever undertake, and if I need to speak to the Director or Violet to arrange it myself, I will. This is about the safety of Eva, and I would have thought you could treat this with some urgency?'

Tony tried to hold his temper in check, knowing his mother had had a shock earlier that day, although she hadn't yet given him the full details. For her to want to meet with everyone personally, and to insinuate that Eva wasn't his top priority... 'Is Eva okay, Mum? And what about you? What exactly happened?'

'We're both fine but it could have been very different. How long before you get here?'

'I should be with you in less than thirty minutes.'

'Good. Well, as the new woman has refused to interrupt the meeting, I need you to give me a contact number for Violet. I'm going to speak to her to see if they can come over on Saturday and I'll explain to you as soon as you get here. Don't worry, Tony, we're fine.' Marion resisted the urge to say *for now*, so as not to worry her son any further.

24

Tony arrived twenty minutes later and listened in shocked silence as his mother calmly explained exactly what had happened at the supermarket. Eva was enjoying her afternoon nap downstairs – Marion didn't want her out of her sight – and Tony tiptoed over to her carry cot and looked at his beautiful daughter. If something was to happen to her … it didn't bear thinking about and he had to force his temper back down in order to be able to think logically and come up with the best solution to protect Eva. What had happened was incredulous, but he believed his mother who would not exaggerate such an incident.

'Do you see why I want to meet with everyone personally now?'

'I do, Mum, and I'm so sorry for not being there when you and Eva needed me. I'll leave the organisation and…'

'You'll do no such thing, Tony. I know there's more to Sunnyfields, than meets the eye, so let's see what Violet says when she calls back and…'

'I'm not sure, Mum, but…'

Marion's phone rang. 'That's Violet now, son. I need to take this call.'

He listened as he heard his mother confirm that the Director and Violet would be able to meet with them on the Saturday, but it would have to be in the morning as the Director had a busy day and wouldn't be able to stay for the barbecue. When she finished the call, Tony was impressed that they realised the urgency of the matter and they both agreed that Tony, Eva and Spike would stay with his mother and Basil until the meeting, for Marion's peace of mind.

*****

The meeting was held indoors at Jim and Fiona's home which was a little bigger than Tony's. Before the others arrived, Jim and Tony moved some of the chairs from the dining room into the lounge so they could all sit in the same room while talking. Tony sat on the settee next to his brother while Fiona pulled up one of the dining room chairs and positioned it near to where her husband was sitting. Marion did the same at the other side with Eva sleeping in her carrycot in-between her chair and where Tony was sitting on the settee. Tony had brought Spike with them and the dog was lying next to Eva's cot. Basil sat in one of the chairs that matched the settee and the other chair was left free for the Director or Violet. The conversations stopped and they all looked at each other in silence.

'I was going to wait until they arrive before telling you all why this meeting is so important. It's not just about what's been happening with Eva, it's...' Marion began, and then the doorbell rang and Spike barked, jumped up and headed for the door.

'Good boy, Spike. Come back.' The dog did as he was told and settled down by Tony's feet, while Jim went to answer the door.

'Thanks for coming,' Marion said, after everyone said hello and Fiona and Jim brought in tea, coffee and biscuits, placing them on the dining room table. 'I'm never sure how much you all know and work on that *need to know* basis, or if you don't actually know what's going on at all?'

'You're not making sense, Mum,' Jim interrupted.

'I'm trying to gather my thoughts, Jim, to make sure you all understand what I want to tell you and it looks like it's having the opposite effect. Let me put it bluntly. Firstly, someone or something wants to harm Eva, and secondly, when I had my near-death experience, I know for a fact that my brain wasn't playing a trick on me. I saw Claire and we had a conversation. I couldn't recall it all at the time or shortly after, but as I've got better and the shock has worn off, it's come back to me a little bit at a time – like when you've been really drunk, and the details of the night before gradually reveal themselves.'

Basil raised his eyes upwards and did his best not to comment, but Marion noticed.

'I know the scientist in you finds it hard to believe me, Basil. But this is something we'll just have to agree to disagree on. I also know that Tony and Jim can sometimes see and hear things that the rest of us can't. They've always had that twin telepathy thing, I know, but since my unusual experience and seeing how Eva reacts to some things I cannot see, I've been watching and making notes.'

She had their complete attention now, and nobody spoke as Marion produced a notebook and started reading from it.

'Let's talk about the telepathy first. You, Tony, know when Jim's going to call and you're going for a run, even if you haven't planned anything beforehand.'

'But that's not telepathy, Mum, that's just routine.'

'Okay, I'll let you have that one. But what about when...let me have a look...' She consulted her notebook and carried on. 'Two weeks ago, Tony told me on the Friday that you were doing a long training session on the Saturday and Basil and I agreed to have Eva and Spike. We came round to pick them up at eight o'clock and were going for a walk first. Do you remember?'

Tony nodded, knowing exactly what was coming.

'You told us your session had been cancelled as Jim had made plans with Fiona, but had forgotten about it. But he didn't call to tell you this until after we arrived.'

'As you said, Mum, we've always had that twin telepathy stuff going on...'

27

'Fair enough, Tony. But I also have a list of dates and times when we've been together, and Spike's warned us that something wasn't right with Eva. Within minutes of these events, Jim has phoned to discuss it with you. How do you explain that? And also, there are far too many things happening with Eva for them to be purely coincidental.'

'Well that's…'

'Never mind for now. Since my death, or near-death experience, and my conversation with Claire, something unusual has happened to me. It's as if all of my senses are heightened and I can feel when there's an uninvited presence in the room. I can't see it, but I know it's there. Also, if I take myself back to when Claire came to me, at other times there's a kind of diluted feeling of that, which means something or someone good is in the room. I can also sense if it's bad because that's how it felt when the evil presence in Eva's mother tried to kill me in the fire in Scotland.'

Everyone had listened quietly. The Director looked around the room, knowing there was no point trying to deny anything further.

'It's time we brought your mother fully on board,' he said, and looked pointedly at the twins. Tony sat back in his seat and sighed, and Fiona squeezed Jim's hand.

Spike opened an eye and looked up and Eva opened her eyes and smiled at the same time. 'Something's in the room,' Marion said, and the twins nodded in agreement.

'Is it…'

'Don't acknowledge you can hear me,' Claire addressed her brothers. 'And be sketchy with the details. I can't talk directly to Mum and it would break her heart knowing that you can communicate with me but she can't. Just tell her that you can sense a presence, that you know it's me, and that you sometimes get messages from me in your dreams and that…'

'Is it Claire?'

'We think so, Mum,' said Jim. 'It's hard to explain but we sense her presence in the same way as you do.'

'And can you speak to each other? Does Claire talk to you? Jim, Tony?'

'She comes to us in our dreams and gives us messages then, Mum.' Jim said, and Fiona tried to hide her smugness at how well her husband had dodged the question.

'We don't talk to her directly,' Tony added, mentally crossing his fingers and hoping that his mother wouldn't suss his lie. Claire was right and they had to look after their mother, even if that meant bending the truth occasionally.

'I knew we were a special family, and it's from my side. It missed my mother but my grandmother…'

'Can we talk about Eva for a moment, Marion?' The Director interrupted. 'I'm sorry to cut you short, and I know it's a Saturday, but we have a meeting in the city later, that's why we wanted an early meeting, and I don't want to rush off today before we all know what's going on.'

'Of course, I'm sorry.'

'Not at all. Now you've mentioned certain abilities within your family and that Eva may have inherited these abilities. We believe your granddaughter is able to see and hear the voices of those no longer with us. She's too young at present to undergo any tests, but we know she has abilities which we have heard about and have tested others for, but none seem to be as pronounced as Eva's. We're unsure whether this is something that most are born with but lose the ability as they grow, whether it's some sort of rare, genetic ability, or a complete fluke.'

29

'I knew it! This all makes sense now. And I think Spike can see the same people or images that Eva can. He has the ability too!'

'We have long believed that many animals can see things that we can't, Marion. And that's why it's important for Spike to be with Eva as much as he can. He can warn us of anything untoward and…'

'Like the incident in the supermarket. But how and why would ants…'

'We have no idea. I've read the report and it was an unnatural event. Whether that was *super*natural or not, I've no idea.'

'I try to find logical and scientific explanations for any unusual events,' said Basil. 'You know I was a non-believer, Marion, and struggle with all of this. But I've been forced to change my whole outlook on life since I've been working for the organisation. The Director showed me the CCTV footage of the incident where something moved you and Eva to safety. I must admit that the only conclusion I can draw is that a supernatural force saved you both. As for the ants, I think that even David Attenborough would have problems explaining them!'

This last lightened the mood a little and they all laughed politely.

'We've taken the CCTV and I'll have it altered. If it's seen as it is, and it goes on social media or to the press, it'll go viral for sure. You'll be hounded and have no peace. So now let's talk about the way forward.'

As the Director continued speaking, Claire attracted the attention of her brothers.

'I've been told that Eva will have a team of guardian angels looking after her. What you would consider twenty-four-hour protection. You don't need to worry about her when you're away working, Tony. I'll come back later and give you more details. Tell them that's what I told you in a dream last night and that she will be completely safe.'

'Tony, Jim? Are you listening?' Marion asked.

'Of course,' said Tony. 'I've just remembered something that Claire told me in a dream. It's a bit weird the way it comes back little by little. But I have no control over that.'

The Director nodded his head for Tony to continue.

'Eva is going to be watched over by guardian angels all of the time and she'll be safe, whatever happens.'

'Is Claire looking after her? Will Claire be with her all the time, Tony?'

'No, Mum.' Marion's face was crestfallen, and Tony's heart went out to her. 'I'm sorry.'

'As long as Eva is going to be safe, and nothing awful happens to her, that's what's important. I don't know what I'd do if…'

Fiona went to her mother-in-law and put her arms around her. 'It's going to be all right, Marion. Eva's got all of us, and real angels, too. Nothing bad is going to happen to her.'

They all agreed and convinced themselves that the special baby would be safe and happy.

The meeting ended shortly after and the Director and Violet said their goodbyes and made their way into the city.

'How do you think that went?' The Director asked his wife.

'We should have told her ages ago when she first came on board. I don't know if she'll ever fully trust us now, or whether she can trust Basil and the twins. There'll always be that doubt about what we're all keeping from her.'

'Perhaps you're right, but what's done is done and we can't change the past. We'll debrief Ryan and

Janine after the next meeting, then we can get away for our break and forget about work for a while.'

'Yeah, right,' Violet chuckled, giving her husband a sceptical look.

*****

Back at Jim's house, they were worried about Marion. 'Are you all right, Mum?' Jim asked, and she recognised the concern on all of their faces.

'To say I'm very disappointed is a major understatement. I lost my only daughter all of those years ago but it turns out that she's been with you both since she died. This changes everything.'

'We lost her too, Mum,' said Tony. 'We were devastated when Claire died and we still miss her.'

'But she sends you messages and…'

'We can't hug her or tease her, and we can't give her a call just to hear her crazy take on things,' Jim said. 'We'll never meet the man she would have married after finding out about…' He stopped, remembering that Claire's fiancée had cheated on her with her best friend. 'We'll never see her children grow, have family get togethers. Every time we plan something as a family I think of Claire and know we'll miss her – even if she's there with us in spirit, or our dreams,' he added, after hearing a cough which didn't come from any of the living people in the room. But he didn't take the hint. 'I know we have Melanie, though we don't see her very often these days, but that doesn't mean we don't still miss Claire.'

Raphael was watching along with Claire and, as her wings drooped and a lone tear dropped from an eye, he hugged her. He also plucked a small feather from one of her wings and put it in his palm. Now, with just one arm around Claire, he gently blew the feather.

It lifted from his palm as if the force of a tornado had moved it, then disappeared.

'Oh look!' It was Fiona who broke their reverie as she pointed upwards. The white feather floating down towards Marion was unmistakable and the eyes of the adults were riveted by its journey downwards, except for Basil who was watching first Spike, and then Eva. They were also looking upwards, but at a place higher than where the feather was on its journey. Eva smiled upwards and Spike wagged his tail gently.

'Thank you, my beautiful angel daughter,' Marion said, as the feather landed in her outstretched hand. 'I'll treasure this forever.' She turned to Basil. 'Shall we go for a walk?' He stood up and held out his hand and they left without saying goodbye to anyone.

Knowing their sister was present, Fiona decided to leave them to it. 'I'm popping to the shops. I don't mind looking after Eva if you two want to go to the gym before the barbecue?'

'Thanks, Fi, I think we'll go for a run,' Jim said, leaning over to kiss his wife, who then left the room.

The twins became serious as they waited for their sister to speak.

Claire had shaken off her melancholy by this stage and was now all business. 'I need to speak to you both about Eva. You must know by now that she's pretty special…'

'I knew that as soon as I saw her,' Tony interrupted.

'I don't mean just because you're her father, Tony. Eva's talents and abilities are rare. So rare, in fact, that others may want to make use of them, and not necessarily in a good way. Your Director was right in that we just don't know for sure how far those talents stretch and how long she will have them. I've already mentioned her guardian angels, and as I said, there'll be a team with Eva all day every day. Unusual, but necessary.'

'You're scaring me now, Claire. Why does Eva need so much protection? Are the bad guys out to get her?' Tony was terrified for his daughter and he wanted to hear what his sister had to say but also needed reassurance.

'You know we all have auras?' she asked, and continued after seeing them nod their heads in agreement. 'Eva's aura is a very bright, startling white, interspersed with flecks of indigo. If you could see auras, you might need to shield your eyes as it's so bright and can be seen from a great distance. Unfortunately, as well as good people, spirits and animals being drawn to Eva, it also attracts those who want to manipulate her powers for their own agenda, even though we have no idea yet what those powers are, or how far they extend. There are also some who are offended by the purity and goodness of her soul, not to mention any weirdo or nutter who may be passing by.'

'Oh no! So, Eva's in terrible danger? And I've just been carrying on my life as normal, when my beautiful daughter could have been attacked or even…'

'Try not to think about it like that,' Jim said, though he hardly believed the words himself. 'You saw the CCTV footage and how Mum and Eva were lifted and moved before the smashing glass landed near them.'

'You're welcome,' said Claire.

'It was you, then?'

Raphael nudged Claire and she had to come clean. 'Let's just say there was heavenly intervention and leave it at that. I know it's going to be difficult for you, Tony, but you have to carry on living your life exactly as you have been. Go to work, come home, and let Mum continue to look after Eva.'

'But how can I, after all you've told me? I'm her father and I need to be with her twenty-four, seven. It's my job to protect her.'

'And you will protect her. But as I said, you're going to need help to do this and Eva will be safe whether you're with her or not. Spike is doing a wonderful job, too, and he's already alerted Mum when there's an unwanted presence. In fact, since her accident, Mum's now tuned in to when there's a presence, whether it's good or bad which has happened since her accident. What she told you was spot on.'

'Was that because she died and came back, Claire?'

'I don't think so, but that's another thing we don't know for sure. Sometimes, when someone has a traumatic experience, it can open areas in the brain that lay dormant. I think this is something to do with our family. It could be that we're genetically predisposed to our psychic abilities more than some other families.'

'You mean like in the same way as genetic diseases, only this could be a good thing?'

'Exactly.'

'As fascinating as all this is,' Tony said, 'my daughter is in grave danger so could we just focus on how we're going to keep her safe? You can't guarantee that she will be safe, Claire, can you?'

'You're right, Tony, I can't guarantee it one hundred percent, but with her family, guardians, and your wonderful dog, anyone who wanted to harm her would have to be very stupid, or mad. They would also have to come up with some ingenious ideas to pull the wool over all of our eyes.'

None of them added that the evils they'd encountered could do all of this.

A look passed between Tony and Jim, and Jim said it out loud, for the benefit of his sister. 'Spike could probably have alerted them to danger in the supermarket, Claire, you know, before the intervention of your… of your, er, people.'

'Exactly. And if the big dog can accompany Eva everywhere, that'll be an extra layer of protection.'

'We'll arrange for that to happen, and the Director will help to get blue badges so that mine and Mum's car can have preferential access to sites and Spike can go everywhere where disability or service dogs are allowed.'

'And if anyone questions it?' Jim asked, playing devil's advocate.

'It doesn't matter,' Tony answered. 'Firstly, it's no one else's business, and secondly, not all disabilities are visual. And despite what you said, Claire, I'm taking some time off work to look after Eva.'

'There's no need, it's…'

'I couldn't forgive myself if anything happened to her and it's a small price to pay to ensure the safety of my daughter. I'm not going for a run today either. I can't leave her at the moment.'

Jim knew it was no good either arguing or trying to reason with his brother, so he didn't say a word.

They said their goodbyes, Claire not adding that if a supernatural being was to come for Eva, there would be very little that Tony could do about it.

*****

The Director gave Tony three weeks before he judged he would be climbing the walls at home; Jim gave him two. Jim was right, and on the weekend following his second week at home, Tony dropped Eva and Spike with Marion and Basil who had agreed to have them for the day. There had been no further incidents since he'd become a stay-at-home father, but this was the first time he had left his daughter and dog since their meeting at Jim's house. Basil watched Tony as he turned at the gate of their house and strummed his fingers on his chin for a few seconds. He walked a few steps back up the path before stopping again, then he turned and went out through the gate, jogging in the direction of Jim and Fiona's home.

Basil smiled at Marion. 'It wasn't easy for him, but he's gone. We can expect him to call throughout the day, but we'll just need to reassure him.'

'No problem,' said Marion, who was already on the floor with Eva's toy box. 'Now which one of these shall we play with today?'

Eva giggled and picked out a car. 'Brrrmmm, brrmm,' Marion thought she said.

'Not a dolly today then, Eva,' her grandmother replied, settling back onto her heels. Basil went to put the kettle on, and Spike lay down with a contented sigh and closed his eyes.

*****

Tony and Jim jogged out from the suburbs into the English countryside. It was their first run in two weeks and Jim noticed his brother wasn't his usual self, fully understanding the reason why. Tony hadn't yet realised that all wasn't well in Jim's world, but Jim could understand that, given his brother's current situation. 'Try to relax, mate, or you're going to struggle.'

'Easy for you to say, you haven't…'

'I know it can't be easy, Tony, but you just have to trust that what Claire told us is going to work. You can't be with Eva all the time.'

'I know that. Let's just get on.'

They carried on jogging and, as each mile passed, Jim noticed the tension disappearing from Tony's body. After eight miles, they were on the outskirts of farmland and used nature's surroundings as their gymnasium. After testing the strength of branches, they did pull ups, push-ups on the ground, hill sprints, squats and jumps. Always competitive, Tony accepted Jim's tree-hang challenge knowing his upper body strength was superior, yet his brother's core strength usually won him the plank challenge. They both dangled from sturdy branches of neighbouring trees chatting and ribbing each other until the lactic acid kicked in.

'I've got a feeling this is going to be my day,' Jim said with a wink.

'Not a chance. I've been training at home and it's only been a fortnight.'

'We'll see.'

After what seemed like an age, Jim noticed Tony's discomfort written all over his face, even though he tried to hide it. Now the ribbing turned to encouragement.

'Hang in there, mate. You can do it. Don't drop yet.'

But Tony's arms started shaking and he knew he was beaten.

'Bollocks!' he said, as he fell from the tree and sat up with a frown on his face. 'That's the worst in ages. I need to up my training. In fact, Jim, I'm bored out of my brains and think I'm going to go crazy if I don't do something about it.'

'Yes!' Jim dropped from the branch and punched a fist into the air.

'Go on, spill,' Tony said, folding his arms and waiting for the explanation.

'The Director thought three weeks, but I said two. He told me to tell you to ring him as soon as you want some work. He's got something lined up for you but wouldn't give me all the details.'

'You're wrong. I'm not leaving Eva.'

'Who said anything about leaving Eva? There's work you can do from home as long as you have all the right equipment. He didn't mention it at the meeting because you needed time to work things out, apparently.'

'Well, you've both got me sussed. I'll give him a call on Monday to see what's what. Shall we get back now and see how Mum and Basil are coping?'

'No way. I know it's hard, Tony, but it'll get easier after today. Trust me on this.'

'I take it you have a plan?'

'Yup. A late lunch then the match. I know they're only in division two but thought we could go and cheer on the town.'

'You got a pass from Fiona?'

'Oh yes. We're all in on *Operation Tony* today. Fi's going to the kiddy petting zoo with Mum, Basil, Eva and Spike and we're all round to Mum and Basil's for dinner and a movie tonight. How does that sound?'

'Yup, sounds great. I just have to make a call.'

Tony did a quick check-in with his mother. 'They're all fine,' he said, putting his phone back in the pocket. Then, looking directly at his brother, he asked the question that had been bugging him.

'What's up with you then, Jim? I know you're trying to hide something but it hasn't worked.'

Jim knew there was no point trying to hide anything from Tony. 'You know Fiona doesn't want kids and that's suited me so far?' he said, not waiting for a response. 'Well now she's decided that she wants to take a break from work and become a foster parent.'

'I see. How long has she felt like this?'

'Couple of months now. I think getting to know Eva has made it more urgent for her. Thing is, I'm not sure how I feel about it.'

'It's a massive decision and both of you have got to want it. Aside from that, how would it work in our line of work?'

'I'm sure the Director could sort that if you decided to go ahead. What are you going to do?'

39

'I told her I'd make up my mind within the next few weeks.'

'Perhaps you need a bit of space from each other to think about it properly. If it wasn't for Eva, I'd suggest a fishing weekend. In fact, maybe we could do that and I'd bring her with me.'

'And you think Mum would be okay with that?' Jim asked, and they both laughed. 'Come on, let's get this done.'

They started the eight-mile jog back, both lost in their own thoughts but for different reasons, each wondering what the future held.

Chapter 5 – Guardian Angels

'Mandy, Dylan and Matthew would be good choices.'

Claire and Raphael were in a meeting with Gabriella and two of the other committee members. In an extraordinary meeting, the committee had sanctioned full guardian angel protection for Eva, and now they had to choose six angels for the job.

'They were on the witch mission with us, Mum,' Raphael said to Gabriella. 'And proved themselves to be brave and quick-witted, with plenty of initiative. Mandy and Dylan are also besotted with each other, so I know they'll do anything to look after themselves, but they're hard workers as well. Matthew has bucket loads of potential and with the right encouragement, he'll go far.

Gabriella ticked their names on her list then they discussed the second team. 'I would suggest Mark, Kim and Trevor. They've worked together before and gel well as a team. We also need Trevor to stop interfering in his sister's life and this may be the ideal opportunity to do so.'

'I agree, partly,' Peter, one of the other senior committee members chirped in. 'But not Trevor. We'll need to find another job for him, he may be too much for a child of Eva's age and I don't think he's quite ready for such a prominent role.'

'So you're ruling him out just because he looks different? Are we…'

'That's enough, Claire.' Gabriella stopped her short. 'I agree with Peter but for different reasons. Trevor, like Matthew, has loads of potential. But unlike Matthew, he hasn't yet been tested and this is too important a mission for that to happen on this job. We need to put him on the reserve list and, like Peter said, find him another role. As soon as he's proven himself, we can add him to Eva's team if…' She hesitated, trying to find the right words. 'Look, I'm sure we're going to need further angels to protect Eva in due course and I want to ensure we give them – Eva and her family – the best chance to protect her. If, in the meantime, Trevor proves himself worthy, he can be chosen later on as a stand-in, temporary or permanent. This is nothing to do with his physical stature. Let's make sure he's worthy of the task first, the same as we've done for the others.

Claire conceded that her angelic mother-in-law had a fair point, so let it go.

'Summon the angels, son, and give them the news and their orders.'

Without further discussion, Raphael and Claire left to do as bid.

*****

Tony had agreed on a sleepover for Eva at his mother's. It was a big deal, but he knew he had to do it if they ever wanted some semblance of normality in their future lives. There was a late- night football match and he was watching it with Jim, while Fiona was out with a few of her girlfriends.

Claire visited her mother's home later that night. Her mother was fast asleep in the nursery but Eva and Spike were awake, looking up at the angels. 'Matthew's one of your new guardians and he will protect you along with the others,' she said to Eva, even though her niece wasn't old enough to understand.

Matthew looked down at Eva and gave her his best smile. The baby recognised the feeling of love, and the anxiety brought on earlier by the presence of the demons disappeared. Eva looked from her auntie to Spike and smiled, then she looked directly at Matthew and did the same. She closed her eyes and was asleep in seconds.

Matthew dropped to the floor in front of Spike and the dog sat up and put his head to one side.

42

'Good boy, Spike,' Matthew said, stroking the German Shepherd. 'You're doing a great job, and with the help of me and my team, we'll protect Eva and keep her safe. She's a very special girl, Spike, and you're special too.'

Spike rolled over onto his back and exposed his stomach, which Matthew tickled. They were going to get on just fine.

'What? What is it?' Marion sat bolt upright in bed. She noticed Spike was lying on his back, eyes closed but tail wagging. Eva appeared to be sound asleep and her initial anxiety turned to calm as all now appeared relaxed and peaceful. *Perhaps Eva or Spike had a dream and made a noise,* she thought as she lay back down, her senses too sleepy to recognise the presence in the room.

'You make my job very easy, Spike,' Matthew said, while he stroked the dog. 'Time for you to sleep now.'

Spike sighed with contentment as he enjoyed the soft caresses and the soothing words. Within seconds he was totally relaxed and in a deep sleep.

Marion slept fitfully for the next hour or so, dreaming of Claire, as she often did when she went back to sleep after waking during the night or early hours of the morning. She got up quietly so as not to wake the baby. Spike opened one eye. Seeing all was well, he didn't wake again until Marion entered the room to open the curtains later that morning, signalling the start of the new day.

Eva was seven months old today! Marion looked at her sleeping granddaughter and tried not to think about the fire and what could have been.

*****

The weeks turned into months and everything was working well with the new arrangements to watch over Eva. Marion was more relaxed and there hadn't

43

been any further nasty incidents since the event with the giant ants in the supermarket. Convinced that they could now enjoy a relatively normal life, Marion wasn't the only one who was becoming complacent.

After a short break, Matthew, Mandy, and Dylan were on their way back to the physical plane for their next stint at guarding Eva. Mandy and Dylan were still in chill mode after their deep sleep, and only had eyes for each other. Matthew shivered with a forewarning that something wasn't quite right. The lovers were a way behind him and slow in recognising the change in atmosphere that he'd felt.

'Dylan, Mandy!' Matthew shouted a warning and turned to look back in their direction. 'Oh my Lord!' he said out loud, as he now recognised the legion of demons barring any escape route for both angels.

'Help us!' Dylan shouted, and Matthew looked on, knowing they were massively outnumbered and there was nothing he could do.

The demons manifested from dark orbs into images of their former selves. One withwho had cruel, dark eyes shouted, 'I have a message from my Lord Satan! The ruler of everywhere!' Then he looked at one of his monster underlings. 'Do your worst.'

The shrieks from the monster and his companions shook the atmosphere as they grabbed Mandy first. She screamed as one of her wings was torn from her back and ripped to shreds. Next the monster pulled one of her arms from its socket and laughed, then licked his lips. Even from the distance, Matthew heard a crunching noise as the demon took a bite out of the limb. He realised their orders weren't even to take them to Hell to live an eternity of misery, but to make them suffer in the here and now.

'Oh Lord, help them!' he begged. Matthew knew that if he stayed, he would be next but if he left, he'd have to live with the guilt that he'd abandoned his team, who were also his friends, for the rest of eternity. It took every ounce of his strength and courage not to flee. Like a soldier in battle, realising this was his last fight, Matthew came to terms with his decision.

Pray for strength then join the battle, he decided. Blocking out Mandy and Dylan's terror and the blood lust noises of the demons, Matthew closed his eyes and prayed for strength, courage and salvation. As he opened them and prepared to cross the divide to join the battle and sacrifice himself, there was a change in the atmosphere.

At the same time, the demon leader stopped watching the horror show of the two angels being ripped to shreds that he considered to be entertainment. He started to cross the distance between the massacre and Matthew, then turned and sniffed the air. As he looked around, he shuddered, trying to see what his senses were warning him about. The demons felt it too, and everything stopped for a nano-second as they all tried to work out what was happening.

Before Matthew could move, a piercing white light appeared, brighter than anything he'd ever seen, and he closed his eyes instinctively.

Two words filled the ether. 'Be gone!'

The light was now a force that hit the demons and the two angels. His eyes were still closed so Matthew didn't see the sudden flames that engulfed all but one of them, and they were gone in less than a second, including Mandy and Dylan. The force then hit him and he was wrapped in love and propelled through the atmosphere faster than the speed of light, not noticing if the dark-eyed demon had perished with his legion or escaped.

Those in the physical world watched in awe as the brightest shooting star ever was witnessed journeying through the night sky.

45

The Committee felt the force and knew something awful had happened.

The Lord left it to Matthew to explain before the great sleep would take the angel out of action for what would be a very long time.

Chapter 6 – Angel Crisis

There was work to be done and the Committee held an extraordinary meeting to discuss what should happen next.

Claire tried to concentrate but was struggling to keep still. Like everyone else she was shocked and upset about what had happened to Mandy and Dylan and wanted to avenge them. She tried to stop the racing thoughts while a broken and exhausted Matthew was asked to explain. The images of Mandy being ripped to shreds were on constant replay in his mind and Matthew stood up and explained.

'It's like he's in some sort of trance,' Claire whispered to Raphael, and Gabriella shushed her.

'And the last thing I saw before the Lord destroyed them was an evil. He was–'

'Take your time, Matthew,' Gabriella said, and they waited for him to compose himself.

'They surrounded them both, made Dylan watch first as they inflicted their worst on Mandy, then their blood lust took over and they started decimating his body, too. They ripped one of Mandy's wings from her back and then … and then, they pulled her right arm from out of the socket. Just like that.' He clicked his fingers, then Matthew's face screwed from remembering the scene and he folded his arms around his body, as if to protect himself. A few seconds later he lifted his head, but his composure had disappeared. Tears streaming down his face, he continued, 'Then one of the more grotesque looking creatures took a bite from Mandy's severed arm. That's when I closed my eyes and started to pray.'

'And then the Lord intervened and they were all destroyed?' Gabriella asked.

'Yes, Gabriella, that's right…' Matthew stopped and thought for a minute, his groggy mind

47

knowing there was something important to be told. 'But there's something else. One of the demons watched without joining in. This one wasn't a grotesque creature like most of the others, he looked like an ordinary man who was on his way to a party or something. I think he was in charge but can't be sure. And when I stopped praying, before the light came, I think he was heading in my direction.'

'Was he destroyed with the rest, Matthew? Think carefully, this is important.'

Matthew's shoulders sagged and he put a hand to his forehead and closed his eyes. They could see he was spent but waited, just in case. 'I don't know. The blast from the light blew me away and I didn't see what happened to him. All I know is that the end must have been sweet relief for Mandy and Dylan. I don't know if I can do this anymore. I've failed my friends and the worst–'

'Go now, Matthew, and rest,' said Gabriella. 'The sleep will cleanse you and will stop you thinking about…'

'It won't bring back Mandy and Dylan though, will it? And if I'd only…'

'If nothing, Matthew. None of us knew these demons were amassing; there weren't any signs and it was a sudden attack. Nobody could have saved Mandy and Dylan. Now you have to save yourself. Simon will go with you.' She nodded to one of the junior angels who approached Matthew and put an arm around him. Matthew was almost collapsing by now and willingly let Simon guide him away.

Gabriella waited for a few seconds. 'Now for the plan of action,' she said, and as she talked, something nagged away at the back of Claire's mind.

'Claire?'

48

She hadn't heard what was said and all eyes were on her. Then it came to her. 'I think I've met the lead demon before, and if I'm right…'

'Answer the question, Claire!'

Raphael leaned over as if to pick up something. 'Should Trevor be in the new team for Eva?' he whispered. Gabriella decided to let it go and waited.

'Oh, absolutely,' Claire said. 'He's strong, determined, and brave, and would be a perfect replacement for Matthew.'

Gabriella put her head to one side.

'Yes, I know he can be very headstrong. But if we … you,' she quickly corrected herself, 'if you decide he's the right angel for the job, it will give him something new to focus on and he won't let you down.'

'Is that your way of saying that he might stop causing problems elsewhere, Claire?'

'That will be a bonus, Gabriella, yes.' They were all glad of a bit of levity to lighten the darkness and most risked a small smile.

'May I tell you something related to the demon who orchestrated the attack?' Claire asked. Gabriella wasn't used to her being so polite so knew Claire must be desperate to tell them something.

'Go ahead but make it quick. We all have lots of work to do.'

That satisfied the other senior angels and Claire took a breath. Raphael held her hand in encouragement. 'When I last visited my niece Eva, there were two particular demons in attendance. One was grotesque and the other presented in the shape of an adult man. He was pleasant to look at until you looked into his eyes. They were filled with darkness and a cruelty that's rare, even for a demon.'

'Get on with it, Claire.'

'Of course, sorry. I didn't think too much about it as they left just as I arrived and before Raphael got there. But the one with the dark eyes made a parting comment. He said, '*Another time. We've plenty of surprises in store for you.*' I thought it was just bravado, you know how they like to have the last word?'

'And your point is?'

'I have a feeling this could be the same demon who destroyed our angels, especially as Matthew, Mandy, and Dylan were all Eva's guardian angels.'

'If you're right, Claire, you know what this means?'

'That Eva's more important to them than–'

'And she's in more danger than even the Committee realised,' Gabriella finished Claire's sentence for her. 'This is now our number one priority. They are not getting that child and she is not coming to any harm.'

'Raphael, I need to speak to Trevor as a matter of urgency. While you find him, Claire, go and speak to your brothers and the other guardians. I want another two permanent teams for the child, but until then we need to protect her from all angles, so do what you need to. Now go.'

They didn't need telling twice and rushed away to follow Gabriella's orders.

*****

Tony was at home on a video call with his brother.

Events in Holland had activated a trigger at the Sunnyfields HQ and had sparked their discussion about a certain bishop in Holland who Eva's mother, Christina, had cheated. As a result of her lies and deceit, the bishop had been found guilty and imprisoned for crimes he hadn't committed. He had also been accused of molesting a teenager when the boy was younger, and although not proven, this had discredited him further. Due to it being a loose end, the trigger had been placed so the Sunnies could monitor the situation with the former bishop and the former teenager who Christina had coerced into lying about the abuse.

While they were on the call, Marion took the opportunity to get some fresh air. 'We're off to the park,' she said to Tony, and waved one of Eva's arms towards the screen. 'Say bye bye to Daddy and Uncle Jim,'

'Bye bye,' Eva said, with another wave of her hand, and they left the house, accompanied by Spike, heading first for the children's play park, and then to feed the ducks.

Some time later, Tony stopped talking and looked around. 'Hang on a mo, it feels like we have a visitor,' he said, and Jim knew straight away who he was talking about.

'Hi, Claire. To what do we owe the pleasure?'

'Eva's in immediate danger,' she said, totally dampening Tony's good mood. 'We all need to take extra precautions until some new measures are put in place to–'

'What do you mean immediate danger? What's happened? Are they in the park? Has somebody–?'

'Nothing's happened to Eva, Tony. But we have, erm, we have… let's call it *intelligence* that something could happen in the immediate future. And because of that I'm doing what I can to help from this side, but I need you guys to up the ante too.'

'I'm going to speak to the Director, Tony, then I'm coming home. I'll call you as soon as I have something extra sorted here,' Jim said.

'You think the Director will…?'

'I know he'll give us extra protection for Eva. Go and get Eva, Mum and Spike now. It'll be safer to have her at home until we know more about this. See you.' With that, Jim was gone, and Tony was left staring at the now blank screen.

51

'Jim's right,' Claire said. 'Go and get them and I'll go on ahead.' Seeing how stressed Tony had become, she stopped herself from adding *just in case*, not wanting to make a bad situation any worse.

*****

The dark-eyed demon had returned to his master and received new orders.

It was a good time for the Devil, although he'd lost some of his minor servants, he knew the enemy had had to destroy their own in order to stop the onslaught led by his cousin. At last, William had proved that he could carry out his orders successfully. 'Go and get me some children to play with,' he told him, 'and bend them to your will. I want them all ready for me.'

His cousin didn't need telling twice. He approached the pits of Hell and selected his team at random. Having an idea of what he wanted to do next, he knew his helpers were indispensable – some would return with him, but others would need to take their chances after the job was finished. As long as they weren't too broken to carry out his orders he didn't care about their past or their future. The main concern was numbers and by the time he'd finished, he had an assortment of thousands of weaker evils ready to do his bidding. All were grateful for respite from the torture pits and degradation chambers, no matter how short, and knew that the more pain they inflicted on whoever their victims were, the less they would have to suffer themselves when they were brought back to Hell. There was always hope of a chaotic event in the ether that would enable them to escape an eternity of pain and misery, but after having endured so much suffering, there was little optimism that this would or could ever happen.

*****

Eva was tired after Marion had played with her in the toddler's play park. Marion put her back in her pushchair and they left the play area of the park and walked towards the lake where they could feed the ducks and greedy geese. As usual, a family of ducks followed, getting as near to the pushchair as they could. Even Spike was used to animals trying to gather around Eva and seemed to know instinctively which were safe and those who meant her harm. He walked alongside the pushchair and, according to the signs, was only allowed in this part of the park in his capacity as an Assistance Dog. He resisted the temptation to chase the annoying geese unless they hassled Marion or Eva, then a warning bark always put them back in their place. A mother duck and her family of ducklings neared the pushchair. Eva giggled as the mother duck came right up and looked in at the child. Eva muttered something in baby language and carried on chuntering away to herself. The late summer sun cast its rays on the water and surrounding parkland and Marion stopped for a few seconds to lift her face upwards, enjoying the rare feel of the warm sun on her face. The moment was broken when she felt something on the bare skin of her forearm.

'Ouch,' she said, as she felt the small drop of acidic venom doing its work. She slapped the insect, but as the first disappeared, so another landed, then another and another.

Marion felt a sharp stabbing pain on her left forearm and looked down. 'Aarggh,' she shouted. Spike barked and Eva started to cry. Marion hesitated for a second as she looked at the insect. It appeared to be a giant ant, like those she remembered from the supermarket, but this one had wings. She tried to brush it off, but it was as if it was glued to her arm. She eventually managed to remove it, but it had left a swollen red welt where it had bitten or stung her. Not having seen such a large flying ant before, it gave her the creeps and Marion shivered involuntarily. Then she

53

saw people on the bench they were walking towards, pointing off into the distance. There was a dark cloud accompanied by a buzzing noise. The people rose from the bench and hurried away in the opposite direction. As the cloud neared, a few of the insects flew ahead of it. Two landed on Spike and he yelped as the large flying ants attacked him.

'Hell's bells,' Marion said out loud, looking around for an escape route but finding none. There was only one thing for it.

'In the water, Spike,' Marion ordered, but the dog hesitated, not wanting to leave them both. 'Go on, Spike, go!' Marion raised her voice, aware that the Spike couldn't do anything to help. This time he did as he'd been told, and took a run and leaped into the water, causing a number of birds to squawk and take flight in panic. Marion tried her best to focus. A middle-aged couple who were also enjoying a stroll tried to assist but the insects ignored them and there was nothing they could do. The man took his phone out of his pocket and made a call.

Another cloud hovered above Eva, then lots of the insects landed on her and the baby started to scream and writhe in the pushchair. Marion noticed red patches appearing on her granddaughter's arms and knew there was no time to hesitate. She lifted Eva out of the pushchair.

'I need you to be brave for Nanna,' she said. Knowing this was no ordinary attack, she also knew she needed help. 'Help us, Claire,' she said, before taking a short run, a deep breath, then jumping in the water.

The ants swarmed around their heads and Marion used one hand to close Eva's mouth as she ducked them both under the water. As soon as they came up for air, the ants were on them and it became a game of cat and mouse, trying to grab as much air to breathe, and to minimise the number of bites to their faces as they bobbed under the water and came back up for breath.

When onlookers realised they were safe and only the woman, child and dog in the water were under attack, a crowd gathered, calling for Marion to get out of the water. A man jumped in and swam to them. He held Eva as Marion ducked her head under the water, then she took Eva from him and ducked her under the water. The insects attacked the stranger, but he endured the danger in order to help them.

Tired, and in pain, Marion knew she wouldn't have been able to carry on without the man's help. She was also able to lean on Spike and realised as he must have been treading water so she could do so. As she lifted her head up from under the water, she took a breath, preparing for the onslaught of insects and to dip Eva under. Even with so much going on, she noticed a small twister in the distance.

'Someone help us for God's sake!' she said, believing it was a force of evil. But she was wrong. She felt an invisible pressure and was pushed under the water, along with Eva, Spike and their helper. They all felt a ripple above them, and this time when they came up for air, there were no insects. The twister was spinning on top of the water taking with it the army of flying ants.

Now the people on the riverbank were staring, open-mouthed but Marion was more concerned about Eva than the extraordinary events of the last few minutes; she'd have time to think about those later. Eva was shaking but quiet and Marion knew they'd take a while to recover from this. As the man swam to the shore with Eva, Marion and Spike followed, and she was helped out of the water by some of the onlookers. As the middle-aged couple put jackets around Marion and Eva, Marion noticed the red marks on her granddaughter's face and knew, from the pain she felt, that she, too, was covered in bites. Spike joined them, and after the big dog had given his body a good shake, Marion noticed red welts on his head, despite the thickness of his fur. 'I've called an ambulance,' a man said, and they heard the sirens approach.

'Go home, Spike,' Marion said, as, assisted by paramedics, she climbed into the ambulance with Eva in her arms.

By the time Tony arrived on the scene, they were already on the way to the hospital. 'What happened?' he asked a policeman.

'A woman and child were attacked by some gigantic flying ants, apparently, sir.' It was clear the policeman thought the reports were exaggerated.

Before he could say anymore, his sister interrupted. 'It wasn't pretty, Tony, and they were terrified, but they're going to be okay. They're on their way to hospital. Spike's making his own way home, by the way.'

Tony thanked the policeman and walked away. 'I don't know how much more of this we can take, Claire.' He rubbed a hand over his face in distress.

Even though Claire had impressed on Tony that Eva and their mother's injuries were not life-threatening, he had an urgent need to be with his daughter to comfort and protect her as much as he could, and also to reassure his mother that everything would be okay – even though he wasn't sure of that himself. He was now determined not to leave Eva for the foreseeable future, even with those she loved.

'I need to get to the hospital,' he said, and started jogging back towards his car.

'Stop running. You have a small job to do first,' Claire replied. 'Those teenagers on the bench next to the willow tree.'

Tony slowed to a stroll and looked towards the willow tree at the riverbank. Half of its branches leaned over into the river.

He wasn't interested but knew Claire wouldn't give him any peace. 'Yes, I see them.'

'Well, the one in the blue top videoed the whole event and wants to post it on social media. If he does that, Mum and Eva's faces will be in the public domain and the last thing we need is any more interest in the unusual events that Eva has had to endure so far in her short life.'

Even in his distressed state he knew his sister had a fair point. 'I agree,' he said, discreetly checking the whereabouts of the policeman and woman as he did so. There was a circular path around the lake, and they were talking to two people quite a distance away from where the teenagers sat. Tony also noticed a gap in the hedge behind the bench about twenty metres away from it.

'Leave it with me,' he muttered to his sister. He needed to get this done quickly so he could get to the hospital. Tony put up his hood and broke into a gentle jog, occasionally punching the air, right, left, right, as he jogged so that to anyone watching, it would appear he was practising his boxing skills and attempting to improve his fitness.

One of the teenagers looked up, but only briefly, until his friend nudged him and showed him something on his phone. They both laughed and the boy holding the phone moved it this way and that trying to get a bigger picture on the screen.

Tony sprinted the few steps and grabbed the phone. Before the teenager knew what happened, Tony had jumped over some plants behind the hedge and squeezed through a gap. Then he doubled back in the opposite direction to where he believed they would look for him. A few minutes later, he was at his car and

57

replaced the hoody for a fresh top from the boot where he always kept one, just in case.

'Good job. See you soon,' his sister said, then he sensed she was no longer with him. He headed in the direction of the hospital but pulled into a layby after driving for five minutes. He checked the phone and discovered the video hadn't yet been posted anywhere. But Tony paled when he saw what his mother, daughter and even poor Spike, had endured. Pulling out into the traffic, he broke all speed limits to get to the hospital as soon as he could.

*****

The Director was in his office reading the report from the Sunny, formerly SAP, Training Section in Brecon. Dee Benson was doing well on the course and keeping up with many of the male trainees. What she lacked in physical strength she made up for in determination and most reports so far were excellent, though he noted that she could be strong-willed and stubborn. *What woman isn't*, the Director thought, and he chuckled to himself knowing he'd be accused of political incorrectness if he voiced his thoughts. He stopped laughing as he read the report of what had happened two days earlier, on the last day of the course's skiing trip in Austria.

Dee Benson was a talented skier and had been on the black slopes with two of the other trainees. It was reported that those at the bottom of the slope heard a rumble from above and looked up. A wall of snow approached the three; the two male trainees were hit and disappeared in the avalanche. The extraordinary witness reports said that Staff Sergeant Dee Benson had been thrown high into the air, clear of the path of the approaching avalanche. The personnel who had witnessed the incident were all trained soldiers; some were very highly trained special operators whose judgement would not have been clouded by panic like that of some untrained personnel. At least some of these people knew how to record events so that their brains would be able to recall exactly what had happened, and they could report back to whoever they needed to. He shuffled the papers. So, the information he'd been given before she'd started training had most likely been true and not exaggerated – as some soldiers were also prone to do – as he'd thought at the time. The decision he had to make now was how to best use the woman's skills and if there was any way his organisation could use her invisible helper as a force for good.

A knock on the door interrupted his train of thought.

'Come.'

Jim entered, his face ashen.

The Director knew it wasn't good news. 'Take a seat and tell me what's happened,' he said, without preamble.

'My mother, Eva, and Spike are in immediate danger. Claire told us-she has some sort of … some sort of intelligence from her side that Eva's going to be under attack. My mother's taken them to the park. Tony's gone straight there, and hopefully, with divine intervention they'll-' He didn't finish the sentence as a vivid mental picture of all the awful things that could happen to them filled his head. 'I need to be there.'

'You're right. Go and help your family and keep me updated as soon as one of you can. I'm going to get extra protection for your niece on a twenty-four-hour basis.'

'Thanks, boss,' Jim said hurriedly, getting up to leave.

'And, Jim. I'm sure Eva and your mother will be all right if your sister and her helpers are involved.'

'I hope so,' Jim said, before leaving the office.

As soon as he left, the Director made a call to his directing staff in Brecon, currently headed up by Ryan, and then he phoned Violet. 'Hello, darling. Yes, I'm fine but there's an emergency. Something, or someone, is after little Eva again, and we need to help them. I have some ideas which I'll explain later and need to go to Brecon. Can you arrange a helicopter?'

'I take it you want it now?'

'But of course, darling. Fancy a trip and I'll explain later?'

Violet heard the concern in his voice, despite his attempt at humour. 'I'll call you back when it's sorted. I'll arrange my pick-up from the flying school,' she said, knowing it would take her about fifteen minutes in the car to get to the school north of the common, and only so long due to the amount of traffic in the South East.

They ended the call and Violet made the arrangements. She left twenty minutes later after taking a shower and choosing some appropriate work gear to wear, which helped to get her mind back into business mode.

Violet parked up at the school, and as she approached the Helipad, heard the sound of the rotors. There was little conversation on the journey due to the noise and the fact it wasn't appropriate to discuss work matters in such an environment, so they enjoyed the countryside below and arrived in Wales ninety minutes after the Director had made the call to Violet. Ryan was at the Helipad to meet them in Brecon, and they were straight down to business as soon as they got into the car.

'Eva and Marion have been attacked again,' the Director started, although Ryan was already aware of the situation.

'Oh no! What happened? Are they all right?'

'They were–'

'Tony phoned, boss, while you were flying.'

'Go ahead.'

'Giant ants again, but this time the flying variety. They have some nasty bites which are being treated, but no long-term physical damage. They're being treated with antihistamines and various lotions and potions. Eva was very distressed and it's a lot of pain and discomfort for a child that age so they've given her a mild sedative so she can sleep and recover. Marion's very shaken, understandably, but other than that, the medics believe they'll both make a complete recovery and have no lasting damage. The main concern is Basil's. He isn't sure how Eva's mental health is going to be affected by these attacks. Although everyone knows how special she is, she's also still a baby, and this sort of constant trauma isn't normal – not for children in this part of the world, anyway.' He added the last, knowing not all families were as fortunate as most in the first world.

'Of course. Nothing about Eva and her circumstances are normal, so all we can do is give her the best protection that we have to offer, and that's why we're here today,' the Director replied.

'Do tell,' said Violet.

'You know the Army staff sergeant I mentioned to you, Vi?'

'Dee someone?'

'Dee Benson. Yes. Well, she's doing the course at the moment and she thinks she's going to be part of an extremely secret part of the Army. I'm going to recruit her to be Eva's bodyguard.'

'Okay.' Violet gave him a curious look. She knew her husband well enough to figure this woman had to have something special to be selected as Eva's bodyguard when none of them knew her. And the way he'd said *going to* instead of *want to* recruit her meant that he was determined to do so. 'Spill the beans.'

'Dee Benson has been involved in some major accidents and incidents during her twenty–nine years on the planet, but specifically during the last seventeen years. Most of which would have killed other people.'

'Sounds like she's extremely lucky–or is there something else going on?'

The Director and Ryan smiled at each other, knowing that Violet had more or less worked out the answer for herself. The Director nodded to Ryan.

'Violet, we think someone on the other side is looking out for her, and that's either her parents or her brother. We'll get the twins to ask their sister but in the meantime, Dee Benson would make a great Sunny and be an asset to our organisation without taking into consideration any of the *special* intervention. But as someone up there is determined to keep her from harm, it can only benefit Eva. She's the ideal fit for the job.'

'Let's hope Ms Benson agrees with that logic,' Violet said, as they arrived at the training establishment. Ryan put the windows down so the gate guards could check their identities. Satisfied, they were waved through the outer perimeter. The Director quickly explained the avalanche incident to Violet.

'She might still be suffering from the shock of it, Vi, it's only been two days. So just bear that in mind.'

'Okay, and what of the two who were injured?'

'They were rescued very quickly, thankfully. One has a broken leg and was discharged from hospital earlier today, and the other was checked over and is now on leave. They were all due to go on leave today anyway, and if Dee accepts the assignment, her fellow trainees will be told that she withdrew herself from the course.'

'It's hard to believe anyone would do that when they only have one term left,' Ryan said, 'but it has happened once or twice before, and the trainees won't know any different. But there's a lot of speculation about Dee Benson. Word got around the intelligence gathering military community before she arrived because she was the only one who escaped injury during the last op she was on.'

'Divine intervention again?'

'Yes, Vi. But we're well placed to know if anyone tries to do any digging. And also, the only ones who will know the truth are the two others we're looking at recruiting if they carry on as well during their final term. And even then, they won't be recruited for the *Specials* wing, so will only know that she works for us, and that's only if their paths cross during future missions or training.'

They arrived at the inner perimeter and the soldiers who were passing by assumed they were high-ranking visitors to the Special Ops facility. It was the only building that was guarded and most people took little notice. The Brecon Beacons were used by a large part of the British Army and trainees on the various courses were used to people coming and going.

'We're going to recruit Dee Benson and my job is to convince her if she doesn't want the job in the first instance? Is that right?'

The Director nodded to his wife and the three walked into the building. The other trainees from her course were getting ready to go on two weeks' leave or had already dispersed and Dee was in the administration headquarters of the training wing, waiting outside Ryan's office. She stood up to greet Ryan and to meet the two civilians who were with him.

'This is Violet and this is the Director,' Ryan said, and they all shook hands.

'Director?' Dee asked, looking to each of them in turn.

'All will become clear,' the Director said, as Ryan swung his arm, indicating they should enter his office.

'Please take a seat,' Ryan said. He took some small bottles of water out of the fridge in the corner of his office and put them on the table around which they were all sitting. 'Help yourselves.'

Dee opened a bottle and took a swig, to give her time to compose herself and study the two newcomers. They had an air of authority about them and could have been military, but she wasn't sure.

'So, Staff Sergeant Benson,' the Director began. 'We're here to offer you a job. A job that's unlike anything you've ever experienced in your time in the Army, or as a civilian before that. Before I give you any details, you need to know that this project is at a higher level than top secret, and on a strict need-to-know basis. You are not permitted to discuss it with anyone outside of those you'll be working with, if you accept the role. Do you understand.'

'Yes.' Dee frowned and looked at each in turn, then she sat up straight in anticipation of what was coming next.

'You have the option now of hearing more and deciding whether you want to take the role, or of telling us that you wish to carry on with your course and join another branch of the military special forces. If the former, I need you to sign some papers agreeing not to discuss our visit with anyone.'

'You do know that I'm in the Intelligence Corps and already subject to the highest levels of security, even beyond top secret?'

'We are aware of that, Dee, yes. I would expect you to already understand that you don't know all of the country's secrets and that we all work on the *need-to-know* principle.'

'Fair enough.' Dee reddened and, suitably chastised, took a few moments to think about what she wanted.

'Okay, I'm ready to hear what's on offer. What do I need to sign?'

The Director nodded towards Ryan who walked to one of the walls and removed a picture. He keyed a number into the safe underneath; a buzzing noise filled the air and the door opened. He took out a file and handed it to Violet. Dee watched as Violet took two lots of papers – each containing three sheets and stapled separately – from the top of the pile, put others to one side, and took a few more sheets from towards the bottom of the file. She handed some of the papers to the Director then slid the two stapled documents to Dee.

'You'll see that the first document is an enhanced version of the Official Secrets Act. Please read and sign. The second is the questionnaire that all of our potential Sunnies are required to complete. We already know a lot about you and your circumstances, Dee, including the tragedy that happened to your family when you were twelve years old. But this will confirm that our information is correct and that there aren't any skeletons in your closet. We also need to know about your medical and financial history. You don't need to complete that one today, just the first one please.'

'It says here that this applies for my lifetime and that any breach *will* not *could* result in a prison sentence. Has anyone from your organisation been imprisoned as a result of a security breach?'

'We are very rarely wrong about people who join our organisation,' the Director answered. 'But on the odd occasion that we are, the individual has been punished commensurate to the crime committed.'

'That doesn't really answer my question.'

'As I said, we work strictly on a need-to-know basis. Nobody is coercing you into working for this organisation, which you'll find out more about after you sign the papers. And then, when you do know a bit more, if you decide you don't want to join us, we can forget about this meeting and you can carry on with your life.'

'Just one more question before I sign. Is your organisation part of the military? Would I need to stay in the army to do the job you want to offer me?'

The Director resisted the urge to say that was actually two questions. 'No and no,' he answered briefly.

Dee signed the papers, stood up and handed them to Violet, then sat back down.

'Would anyone like some coffee before we begin?' Violet asked. The atmosphere was more relaxed when she returned with the drinks and her husband asked her to make a start.

'I'm going to tell you what we already know about you, Dee, and why we want you to come and work for us, but first, let me tell you a bit about us.' She smiled. 'Our organisation is twofold. You already know this is where we run our courses, but we also have on-the-job training for our successful recruits – call it an apprenticeship if you like – which can take up to two years to complete depending what we want from that particular recruit, and what he or she has to offer us. Our successful recruits go on to complete missions that are run by my husband, the Director. Ryan here is one of our team, and you already know that he's part of the Directing Staff here in Brecon. But he also carries out missions and–'

'What sort of missions?' Dee interrupted.

'We'll get to that,' the Director replied before Violet continued.

'Another part of our training wing is for those with unusual talents or abilities, or those who have been brought to our attention due to paranormal activities.'

'Paranormal?'

'Yes, Dee. Your military skills are good enough for you to be recruited to our organisation, but when the paranormal element is added, you are a perfect fit for the job we have lined up for you.'

'I didn't realise that anyone knew about the strange–'

'What we know about you, Dee, is that your parents and brother were murdered in a school shooting, along with eight others, when you were just twelve years old; that there were problems with your estranged aunt and uncle, and that you were fostered until you decided to join the army at just seventeen years of age. We also know that the first recorded paranormal event occurred when you were thrown out of the pathway of a number of bricks that fell from a building site when you were fifteen years old, and that the girl you were with suffered a broken arm, cuts and bruises and a concussion. There may have been others before then but that's the first recorded incident.'

'All the others are here,' the Director said, picking up the papers Violet had handed to him, 'including the last one before the avalanche, two days ago.' He passed the papers across the table to Dee. 'I'm now going to ask you what your take is on these paranormal events. Bearing in mind the nature of our organisation, I would appreciate your complete honesty.'

Dee looked at all three, with a pained expression as if she were struggling to come to a decision. Then her expression changed, and she took a leap of faith.

'I guess it's in for a penny, in for a pound,' she muttered, taking a deep breath. 'I'm going to be totally honest with you all now and you will probably think I'm crazy and decide you don't want me to work for you after all.' They waited without comment, so she continued. 'My brother, Trevor, always called me his little sister even though I was a lot taller than him. He was born with dwarfism, and as far as I can remember, I was always taller. I was teased in primary school, and bullied at one stage, and Trevor came to my rescue. He told me then he'd always look after me and I believed him. My take on these events is that Trevor's still looking after me, even though he's been dead for the best part of seventeen years.' She sat back in her chair and folded her arms, waiting for the onslaught.

'Does Trevor talk to you?' Violet asked.

'Don't be daft,' Dee said, laughing. She stopped when she saw none of the others were joining in. 'No, he doesn't talk to me. But I'm convinced it is Trevor that looks after me when I'm in trouble. He's saved me from injury, or even death, loads of times. There's been other occasions, not just these,' she added, lifting the papers and waving them.

'The job we would like you to consider is bodyguard to a very special little girl.'

'Bodyguard?'

'You know how Trevor helps you?' Violet asked, and Dee nodded. 'Well imagine paranormal events where someone was trying to hurt you, or somebody else.'

'But why would they?'

She missed the almost imperceptible nod the Director gave Violet before she continued. 'You've been honest with us and I appreciate that and now we're going to return the favour. You need to know what we're up against and the potential dangers involved.' Violet leaned forward on the table towards Dee. 'This little girl, who's not yet one year old, has abilities and talents that we can't yet fathom. Someone, or something, on the other side wants to harm her, in the same way that someone, sorry, Trevor, on the other side, wants to protect you.'

'But how am I supposed to protect her from an invisible enemy? That would be impossible, as well as scary.'

The Director, Violet and Ryan shared a look and a smile.

'Am I missing something here?' Dee asked.

'You protect her,' said the Director, 'with the help of your brother. If you are looking after Eva and he sees you getting into trouble, by saving you he'll also save Eva.'

'The reason you want me for this job is because of my dead brother's skills, not mine,' Dee said flatly and it was a statement rather than a question.

'I'm not going to lie to you, Dee. That was the main reason, yes. But we would have offered you a role in the organisation anyway, just not in the SAP Section.'

'Sap?'

'It's what we call our Special Abilities Personnel. But we're all called Sunnies as well.'

'Sunnies? Hang on, never mind that–do you mean there are others who have had similar experiences to mine?'

'There are,' Violet answered this time. 'We can't tell you any more until you decide whether you're going to take this job.'

'Would I get to meet some of them?' she asked, ignoring Violet's comment.

'Yes, you would.'

For the first time since her brother had started to come to her rescue, Dee felt there was a chance she could be totally honest with people and that she wouldn't be the odd one out that weird things happened to. 'I might get to walk into a room without everyone going quiet or staring at me,' she said. 'Or not be the only one considered a weirdo.'

They waited patiently while she contemplated her future.

'But I'd have to expect the unexpected and what if I couldn't protect the child? What if something happened to her on my watch? How could I ever forgive myself?'

'You could ask yourself all of these questions,' the Director replied. 'Or you could say that if you take this job, with the help of your brother, you are giving this child the best chance of protection that she is likely to receive. Do you want a few days to think this over?'

'No. I'll do it. When do I start?'

*****

While the Director, Violet and Ryan were busy recruiting Dee Benson, Tony was at the hospital with his mother and Eva. The bites were tormenting them both and they were covered in hydrocortisone cream which doing little to ease their discomfort. A nurse was on one side of Eva, monitoring her condition, and her grandmother had left her own bed and was sitting on the other side, holding her granddaughter's hand. She didn't see Tony approach and, not wanting to make her jump, he called, 'Hello', from the door.

'Oh, son, it was awful!' Marion said, standing. Tony took his mother in his arms and hugged her, noticing that his daughter was sleeping peacefully. 'Ouch, careful!' she said, as she loosened the hug. 'I've never seen ants so big and nasty and…'

The nurse looked up. Tony sent his mother a warning look not to say anything else, not realising that it was too late.

'How's my daughter doing?'

'She was in a lot of pain and discomfort, so we gave her a mild sedative and some other medication to calm the bites so she could rest without pain. I've never seen anything like this before, but the doctor tells me both your daughter and your mother…' the nurse smiled towards Marion, '...will make a complete recovery. We kept an eye out for any allergic reactions as it seems that the ants that attacked them were unusual, to say the least, but that hasn't happened and it's unlikely that it will now. The doctor's contacted the London School of Hygiene and Tropical Medicine and an entomologist should be with us shortly.'

'Why an entomologist? Did someone keep specimens of these unusual ants? Surely it's just because we've had a few unseasonably hot days, isn't it?'

'I don't know about that, Mr Sylvester,' the nurse said, looking at the name on the card at the bottom of Eva's small bed. 'You may want to speak to the doctor and entomologist. For the time being, we'd like to keep Eva in overnight to monitor her condition, just to be certain she doesn't have any other reactions to this unusual attack.'

Tony wanted to take his daughter home, wrap her up in cotton wool and the security of their four walls, and never let her out again. Unfortunately, he knew this wasn't possible and that the hospital was the best place for Eva until they were sure there were no long-term consequences as a result of the attack. Physical consequences, he corrected himself mentally, hoping she would be too young to remember the awful things that had already happened to her in her short life so far.

'Please call me Tony,' he replied, before continuing, 'and keeping her in overnight is a good idea. Eva has an assistance dog–I take it he can stay here with her, as well as me?' It was the first time Tony had thought about Spike and now he started worrying about his dog, knowing he was likely to need treatment and some TLC too.

'I'll need to check,' the nurse replied.

'And me,' Marion added quickly.

'The doctor said you can go home, Marion, and the GP can monitor you daily. We'll arrange for the District Nurse to call…'

'I can't do that. I need to stay with my granddaughter.'

'You go home, Mum, and let Basil look after you. The Dir… he'll know what's happened by now and will be on the way home. If there's any changes, I'll let you know.' Tony turned to the nurse. 'I need to be able to bring Eva's assistance dog to her. He can…' he hesitated, '…I have sound reasons for needing the dog here. Can I speak to the doctor please?'

'Of course, Tony.' The nurse looked from Tony to Marion, understanding his anxiety after what had happened to his daughter and mother. 'I'll go and find him.'

As the nurse was about to leave, a head popped around the curtain. 'Hello,' Fiona said. 'How is she, and how are you, Marion?'

'This is my sister-in-law, Fiona,' Tony explained to the nurse. 'She's going to be all right but needs to stay in overnight to be monitored and…'

'That's one of the things I've come to tell you, Tony. An entomologist has contacted the hospital and they would like Eva to be transferred to the Princess Margaret hospital in London. As long as she's able to travel.' She looked at the nurse.

'I'll go and speak to the doctor.' The nurse disappeared, wondering what was really going on.

'The Director's arranged a private room for you and Eva, and Spike can stay there too,' Fiona said. 'The hospital has family rooms, so Jim's going to stay tonight, and he said you can each do shifts of two hours on, two hours off to watch Eva, like you do when you're doing your night work. He's also taken Spike to the vets who's given him some cream and a course of tablets. His thick fur only saved him from some of the bites and

72

he's in some discomfort but will make a complete recovery.'

Marion looked from one to the other. 'That makes me feel better, Tony, that you and your brother will be looking after Eva, and that Spike's okay and he's going to be with you both, too.'

Tony knew he'd be awake all night but was grateful for the support and knew he'd feel better with the company of his twin.

*****

The attack on Eva had distracted Claire from finding Trevor and bringing him to the Committee for his new orders. And now Claire, along with Raphael, knew they had to find him to take him to see Gabriella, then come back so he could look after his important new charge. Claire was on edge and wanted to get back to the physical plane as soon as possible to watch over her beloved niece.

Having ignored the telling off from Gabriella when he saved his sister from the avalanche, Trevor was putting some distance between himself and his *crime scene*, and he met Claire and Raphael in the ether.

'Follow us,' said Claire. 'Your presence is requested.'

'Do all of the Committee want to see me or am I to see Gabriella alone? Am I getting sacked? Will I have to guard the roaches in the bat cave? I've done that before and know what to expect. Is it that or could it be something different? Does she know about the avalanche and what happened? How did she find out?'

'Avalanche?' asked Claire, ignoring the barrage of other questions. 'What are you talking about, Trevor?'

'Well, if you're asking me, Gabriella doesn't know about it so it's nothing to do with that! I might not be going to the bat cave after all. Onwards and upwards,' he shouted, lifting one of his short arms into the air, with a closed fist.

'Playing at superhero again,' Raphael said, with a smirk and Claire just shook her head. They caught up with the small man and flanked him for the remainder of the journey.

'Be quiet and don't speak unless you're asked to, Trevor,' Raphael reminded him. 'Do you understand?'

Trevor stepped from one foot to the other, almost bursting with curiosity. He tried to behave himself and nodded at Raphael as they entered the Committee's Chambers.

Everyone inside looked very sombre and Gabriella spoke. 'We have a new assignment and there's a possibility of a promotion in it for you,'

Trevor was unable to contain his excitement. He kept quiet, as Raphael had advised, but clapped his hands then rubbed them together and smiled. Gabriella and the other Committee members gave a small smile. Trevor noticed they didn't share his enthusiasm and he looked around. The atmosphere felt like they were surrounded by black clouds. His good mood dissipated and he spoke, despite Raphael's earlier advice.

'What's happened?'

'I'm sorry to be the bearer of bad news,' Gabriella said. 'But—'

'Is it Dee? Has something happened to my sister?'

'Silence, Trevor!'

The chambers almost shook. Gabriella rarely shouted and everyone looked at her. It did the job; Trevor was shocked into silence. She shook her shoulders, fluttered her wings, and then continued, 'We all love your enthusiasm, Trevor, but your obsession with your sister has to stop. Despite your own opinions, not everything in their world or our world is about your sister. Do you understand?'

'Yes, Gabriella.'

Seeing him staring at his feet and the misery on his face, Gabriella wanted to hug the angel who had the courage and mind of a man one minute, but could revert to an impatient boy the next. It was time to see what he was really made of and she kept her tone serious when she continued. 'The evils have brought darkness to our light and I have some bad news. Mandy and Dylan have been obliterated and Matthew is no longer able to help us in our fight.'

Trevor half-opened his mouth then changed his mind. He bit his lip and Gabriella was unsure whether that was a habit or something he needed to do to stop himself from interrupting. Tears ran down his cheeks as she continued.

'The job I want you to consider is the one that Matthew was leading on. Mandy and Dylan were part of his team. There's a very special little girl that needs protecting in the physical world. The problem is, her star shines so brightly that everyone wants to see her or use her talents. As you can imagine, this is no ordinary task and requires someone with strength, fortitude, and courage.'

'And you thought of me?' He couldn't help himself.

'Yes, Trevor. We all know how determined you can be and how courageous you are. We also know that you might even keep little Eva amused with your antics, as well as helping to protect her. But as I've said, this is a very dangerous job and we're not quite sure whether you have the experience to take it on. What do you think?' They all waited for his response. 'Trevor?'

'I'm sorry. I was taking a moment to think about how Matthew must have felt when you gave him this job. And then when Mandy and Dylan were obliterated – it must have been horrific if they didn't even consider taking them back to the Devil's lair?'

'It was the worst thing that's happened for a very long time,' Gabriella said with a sigh. 'They were attacked by a legion of demons who acted like they were under orders to put them out of action. Permanently. It was so bad that The Lord himself decided to intervene, and unfortunately, he had to sacrifice Mandy and Dylan for the greater good.'

'I can't imagine how awful that was. I hope Matthew is able to recover from it in the passage of time.'

'So do we. But now we must honour the memory of Mandy and Dylan by ensuring we do a good job of looking after the child. Now you know almost as much as we do, and what risks are involved. You may turn down this job and we won't think any less of you.'

Trevor looked around the Committee, each of whom either nodded or mumbled their agreement with Gabriella or mumbled their agreement.

'Do you need time to think it over?'

All eyes were on Trevor and he was unusually quiet while contemplating Gabriella's words. It was a surprise to Trevor that not only did Gabriella seem to like him, but for him to be offered such an important job, she must also rate his abilities. As they watched, he seemed to grow in stature in front of them as he straightened to his full height of four feet.

'I'm honoured that you believe in me and I'll do everything in my powers and ability not to let you down. I also give you my word that I will not leave the child in order to protect my sister – though as you know, it won't be easy for me. I won't let you or the Committee down, Gabriella.'

The Committee broke into spontaneous applause, recognising that the teenager who had walked into the chambers had now become a man.

'I believe that you mean every word you say, Trevor. There's something else you should know. It seems that one particular demon has his eye on the child, and we believe he's been involved in more than one attack on her. We don't know his name, but he presents as a good-looking adult male. You'll recognise him by his unusually dark and cruel eyes. Don't try to fight him on your own because you're unlikely to win. Do you understand?'

Trevor's eyebrows raised briefly. 'I do.'

'Now go about your duties. Raphael and Claire will help you to choose the other members of your team and advise you of the best way to organise them and to protect the child. If you have any questions or need any help, go to them in the first instance–and good luck.'

'Thank you, Gabriella.' He bowed deeply, and she rolled her eyes, laughing at the same time.

'Get going, Trevor.'

*****

Eva was kept in a private room of the hospital for an extra night. She'd undergone all manner of tests and when she was discharged everyone was satisfied that any after-effects of the bites would be mental, and emotional, but not physical. The swellings had gone down, and the red patches where she had been bitten were already starting to disappear. Speedy medical treatment had stopped any infection, despite the best attempts of the demons.

Tony and Jim were shattered, and Spike was restless when the call came from the Director. 'I've got you some help with Eva,'

'I'm not leaving my daughter.'

'I'm not asking you to leave Eva. But you're going to need help and it's all arranged. I'm coming to yours at two pm today, with Violet, Ryan and Eva's extra bodyguard.'

Tony knew he needed all the help he could get and trusted the judgement of his boss, so didn't argue. 'Okay, see you then.'

'Put Jim on, I need to talk to him about a new assignment.'

Tony passed the phone over to his brother and started getting their kit together to go home. He listened to some of the conversation while going about his business.

'An ex-bishop?' Jim said. 'Okay, I'll check it out when I receive the information and let you know this afternoon.'

Chapter 7 – The Bishop's Work

Tony had settled Eva in at home and just finished eating lunch with Jim when the doorbell rang. Jim went to answer it and saw the Director, Violet, Ryan, accompanied by a woman. He tried not to act surprised, knowing he'd been wrong to assume that the new bodyguard for Eva was a man.

'Please come in,' he said, moving out of the way so they could walk through to the lounge in front of him.

'This is Tony,' the Director said to Dee, 'and this is Eva.' He pointed to the sleeping child.

'I'm Jim, Tony's brother,' Jim said, and Dee resisted the urge to say, *no shit?*

They all shook hands and Jim went to the kitchen to get the brews on.

'Dee has agreed to work for you as Eva's new bodyguard,' the Director explained, and Tony studied the woman as his boss talked. Spike had already checked her out, and after she had petted his dog, Spike had decided to lie by her feet. She was of average height and a slim build, so Tony did wonder how she would be able to help to keep his daughter safe from danger. He knew the Director wouldn't have chosen her without good reason so decided to keep quiet until he had all of the information.

'We've taken Dee off the course before the final term and had already decided to employ her as a Sunny…'

Having watched Tony assessing her, Dee interrupted. 'I may not be that big, Tony, but I'm a martial arts expert, used to box when I was younger, and can fight dirty too. As far as a physical presence is concerned, I've got it covered. I can't help when there's a non-physical presence, but I know a man who can…' She smiled.

Tony looked from Dee to the others, knowing they were privy to some information that the Director was yet to share. Jim brought in the refreshments.

'Dee's a martial arts expert and an ex-boxer,' Tony quickly told his brother as they all settled down with their drinks.

The twins looked at each other, and it seemed to Dee that they were sending non-verbal messages, 'Okay, you've got our interest,' Jim said. 'Do tell.'

'Dee's brother, Trevor, died when she was a youngster and it seems he's made it his business to look out for her.'

'I see, but…'

'Not yet you don't, Tony. Dee's brother has moved her out of harm's way on a number of occasions when she would probably have died if he hadn't intervened.'

'Much like…' Tony was about to share the news about the supermarket incident but thought better of it. He stopped mid-sentence.

'As I was saying. It seems that Trevor is intent on helping his sister and therefore, by extension, if Dee is holding hands with Eva for example and something were to happen, we hope that both ladies would be helped by Dee's brother.'

Along with the others in the room, Dee was quick to notice another look passing between the twins. They were fit, in both the traditional and modern context of the word. It was weird seeing two guys who looked like duplicates of each other, and she could only distinguish between them by the different coloured clothes they were wearing–that, and one other thing. She tried to ignore the feeling she had when she looked at Tony, Eva's father, and put it down to the sympathy she felt as a result of all he'd been through with his daughter in her short life.

'We'll agree to it, but only on a trial run where we can terminate Dee's employment whenever we see fit,' Jim said, and turned to Dee. 'No offence, but that's the only way this is going to work.'

Now confused, Dee thought she'd got it wrong. 'Sorry, I thought you were Jim but I've obviously got it mixed up somehow. You are Tony, Eva's Dad and you're Jim?' she nodded towards Tony. 'Is that right?'

'No, you were right in the first place,' Tony said.

Dee looked from brother to brother. 'But Jim just said you agreed to me being Eva's bodyguard, not you, and…'

'Yeah, that's right.'

'But how would…'

'We've all known each other for years, Dee, and sometimes forget it can take a little while for a newbie to get used to the twin thing they have going on,' the Director explained. 'They tend to know what each other is thinking, finish sentences, know if the other is in a spot of bother, know when they're going to phone before they do, always…'

'We are here you know!'

'Okay, Tony, point taken. The job then. It will involve you, and Tony, sharing the care of Eva. And I'm going to ask Fiona to help out, too.'

'I thought you said I was going to help,' Jim said.

'And me.' This was from Ryan and he looked at Jim in confusion.

'That was the plan until earlier today when a few triggers warned me of an operation we may need to mount, depending on the intelligence. I'll talk to you both about that separately. But back to the business in hand. Most of the guarding will be mind-numbingly boring, like most security work, interspersed with moments of high-octane action. We all hope the latter will be few and far between, for all of our sakes. Do you have any questions, Dee?'

'Loads. But I'll ask about the terms and conditions, and admin, such as sleeping and eating arrangements later. My first point is what Jim said earlier. If Tony, or Tony and Jim want to be able to terminate my employment whenever they see fit, I want the same option.'

'Fair enough. Anything else?'

'Shall we say a month's trial and we reconvene at the end of it for a debrief?'

'Sounds like a plan. We'll leave you to settle in now. Call Ryan if you need anything and he'll know how to contact me or Violet.'

'Will do.'

'Now I need to talk to Jim and Ryan so…'

'Shall I spend some time with Eva? Maybe I could take her and the dog…'

'Spike,' Tony said.

'I could take Eva and Spike for a walk if you like?'

'Tony will go with you,' the Director said, in a voice that brooked no argument. Tony, curious about the mission, tried to hide his disappointment at not being included, and Jim was the only one who noticed. He found himself brightening at the thought of getting to know Dee, and not just because she was Eva's new bodyguard. He knew his brother would fill him in on the details of the new mission as soon as he could.

*****

Although Christina, Eva's biological mother, had died in the fire and, according to Claire, the witch who had possessed her wouldn't bother any of them again, there were repercussions from the chaos she had caused. Triggers had therefore been set-up to notify the staff at Sunny HQ when specific actions occurred with people related to the case. One of these triggers was the former Bishop Lange being released from prison, and this is what the Director wanted to discuss.

'Mr Lange, the former bishop who Christina framed, has been released from prison and has also been pardoned.'

'Well that's good to hear,' Jim replied. 'Somebody must have read your report and recommendations?'

'Indeed, Jim. Somebody high up by the looks of it. But it's not all good news I have for you both today. Do you recall that Mr Lange was imprisoned for fraud, not for indecent assault on Ruben Groot?'

Both men nodded.

'It seems that Ruben had a pang of conscience and had been struggling with guilt over the part he played in the former bishop's downfall. He'd been undergoing psychiatric treatment.'

'I suppose, if he's half decent, that was always going to happen. That sort of thing can destroy a person if they let it,' Ryan said.

'I agree. But it was up to Ruben to forgive himself and make amends for his mistake. I hoped he could do so.'

'You say hoped,' Jim said, 'Did he lose his battle?'

The Director nodded sadly. 'Unfortunately, he took his own life. He shot himself in the head, so we know it wasn't a cry for help.'

'How very sad. Another family ruined.'

They thought about Ruben and his loved ones for a moment before the Director continued, 'That woman ruined so many lives, but at least Mr Lange can move on. We're not sure what he plans to do now he's out of prison. He's currently living with a friend, still near Amsterdam, and I should think he'll need some time before deciding on his future.'

'Okay. What do you want us to do?'

'We have a few people in the Amsterdam vicinity. Get them to monitor the situation, Jim, and let me know of any changes. Here's their details.' He handed him a USB stick. 'I'll send the password via secure email later. Any questions?'

'No. It seems pretty straightforward.'

'If we have to move on this one you two will need to work together because of Tony's situation. I've taken you off directing staff duties for the final term of the course, and want you to concentrate on this, with Jim. You need to spend some time together, so you get used to working without Tony. When things calm down here, Tony will do the tech stuff, but we're not sure how long before that'll happen.'

There wouldn't be any further information or questions until Jim had made contact with the Sunnies in Amsterdam and they received some intelligence from there. They said their goodbyes and the Director left to join Violet at Marion's. Jim and Ryan decided to meet up for a fitness session later and left Tony's house shortly after the Director.

*****

Marion met Dee shortly after they returned from their first walk. Both her handshake and smile were genuine and friendly, and Marion warmed to Dee within a few minutes of meeting. Then she only picked up positive vibes when they discussed which way of working would be best for the family. They also talked about whether Dee should share the nursery with Eva and Spike but had agreed that wasn't a good idea. The dog would alert them to anything that happened during the night, or when neither were with Eva.

'If we can't protect my daughter in my own home, there isn't much hope for us is there?' Tony said. It was a depressing thought and they all hoped that the situation would only get better.

84

Two days later, Tony and Dee were still settling into their new routine and trying to get Eva used to Dee. She was a friendly baby but had started to develop anxiety around new people, so it was taking longer than Tony and Marion had expected. She had also become nervous when being taken for a walk in the park, and although Basil had said this was understandable, it was a worrying development.

Dee agreed it was worrying, but quickly settled into the house by keeping herself to herself when she wasn't looking after Eva. Tony was trying to bring a semblance of normality to the situation and was forcing himself to work from home.

One of the things Dee had already done in an attempt to separate her work from her private life, was to join the local gymnasium. She was happy to work out on her own, but knew that if she joined a few organised classes there would be more chance of meeting new friends.

There hadn't been any incidents in the short time since she'd started the job and Dee was in her room, hurriedly dressing in her sports kit before making her way to the Spinning class at the gym. She'd lingered over breakfast and hadn't kept an eye on the clock when playing with Eva, so knew she'd miss her first class if she didn't hurry up. She heard some noise downstairs and listened.

'Only me,' Marion called, as she opened the door.

'Is Dee down the gym,' she asked, as Tony greeted her and Eva clapped her hands in delight at seeing her Nanna.

'Hello, my beautiful girl,' she said to Eva, scooping her off the floor and into her arms. 'Whoo, you're getting a bit heavier! Who's Nanna's best girl then? What are you up to?'

Dee was coming out of her bedroom and about to call hello from the landing when she heard Marion carry on.

'Do you like your new friend, Eva? Nanna does, and so does Daddy. We think Daddy likes her a lot, don't we Eva?'

'Give it a rest, Mum, and Dee isn't in the gym, she's…'

'Oh heck. I'm only teasing son.'

Feeling her face redden, Dee snuck back into her room. She waited for a few minutes before rushing down the stairs. 'Hi, Marion. All good?'

'All well in my world thanks, Dee. How are you settling in?'

'So far so good. Eva was a bit better with me this morning so we're getting there. Sorry, I must rush. Don't want to miss my class unless I have to.'

Tony watched as they spoke, relieved that Dee hadn't heard his mother's comments.

She took her bag off the hook and put her phone in her pocket. 'Bye, see you all later.' She waved at them all and opened the front door. As Marion said goodbye and turned to take Eva into the lounge, Dee looked directly at Tony and winked, then smiled.

She did hear, he thought, and more importantly, she wanted him to know that she'd heard his mother's words.

When Dee returned less than two hours later, she showered and accompanied Marion and Eva to the shops. It was the first time his daughter had been out of the house without him since coming home from hospital. Tony stood up from the computer and walked to the window. Nothing new in their quiet cul de sac. He sat down at his desk again and looked at the document on the screen. Five minutes later, he read the same email for the nth time, and the information still hadn't gone in. He moved his head from side to side, cricking his neck as he did so, then had a long stretch. *No good sitting here doing nothing*, Tony thought, knowing it would be easier to distract his worrying thoughts if he did something practical. Deciding to get into scruffs and tidy up in the garden and garage, he felt a change in the atmosphere and knew he had company.

'Claire. Has something happened? Is Eva all right?'

'Nothing's happened,' she quickly told her brother. Though they hadn't been to see Eva, there was no evil presence lurking and the angels knew that nothing untoward was going on.

'Eva has a new team of guardian angels looking out for her, and we're confident they can deal with anything unusual that may happen in the future.'

'I've heard that before, Claire.'

'Awful things happen that I can't control, Tony. But that doesn't mean I'm not doing everything in my power to…'

'I'm sorry. It's just that…' He rubbed a hand through his hair and Claire didn't have to look hard to see that the worry had put extra years on her brother. She wasn't allowed to tell him about the specific presence who seemed out to harm Eva, and knew that all they could do was to give her as much protection as possible and look out for her as best as they could. That wouldn't inspire confidence in any father whose daughter was in danger. She wondered if ignorance was bliss under these circumstances and her heart went out to her brother as she contemplated the situation.

'I can only imagine the fear and worry you're going through. Eva's new number one angel is clever and determined.' Claire ignored Trevor's posturing as she told Tony about his talents. 'He's also fun, though only when the occasion arises,' she added quickly, 'and I think that Eva will love him…'

'I thought you were Eva's number one angel, Claire?'

'I'm Eva's number one auntie, Tony and…'

'Can't you be with her all of the time? Why does it have to be somebody else?'

'I would if I could, Tony. You must know that. But the main thing is that Trevor would risk his own existence in order to protect Eva, and we can't ask for more than that.'

'I suppose that will have to do then, won't it?' Tony said, and Claire watched Trevor's reaction at the ungrateful words of her brother. The little man almost shrunk in front of her eyes.

'We all want what's best for Eva and if you knew what sacrifices had been made on this side as well as your side, you might just be a little more grateful,' Claire said. 'I know it's not easy, Tony, but it's not easy for us either.' She left with a whoosh and was quickly followed by Raphael, with Trevor bringing up the rear.

'I know and…' Tony stopped as he realised his sister had already gone, and he felt even worse than he had earlier.

*****

The autumn sun beat down as they crunched the leaves underfoot. Marion chatted easily to Dee as they headed towards the lake in the park and watched as a few of the ducks waddled over to have a peek at Eva. Marion was used to it but it surprised Dee.

'Animals always want to be near her,' Marion said. 'I was surprised, too, the first few times but now it seems perfectly normal.'

'That's amazing. I've never seen anything like it…'

Their conversation stopped abruptly as Eva let out a loud cry, and then bawled her eyes out as they approached the lake to feed the geese and ducks. It was so out of character, and she sounded so baleful that Marion stopped and scooped her up into her arms.

'We're going to be okay, baby girl. Nanna and Dee Dee won't let anyone hurt you.'

Dee rolled her eyes at her new nickname but then smiled at them both. 'Shall we see if the ducks want some seeds, Eva?' she asked, but Eva grizzled in reply and even the rustling of the bag which held the seeds and some dried fruit for the birds didn't pique her interest and did nothing to improve her mood.

Marion felt a subtle change in the atmosphere and looked around. Seeing the look of concern on her face, Dee immediately went onto high alert. She checked the surrounding areas and was ready to take Eva to head off to one of the escape routes she'd already earmarked while out running the previous day.

Then Eva stopped crying and looked above and beyond her grandmother's head. She looked back at Marion for a second, looked up again and smiled, then giggled. Both women noticed that Spike had sat down and was also looking in the same direction as Eva, tail thumping on the ground.

'Is everything all right?' Dee asked.

'Couldn't be better,' Marion said, and her expression of concern changed to one of peace. Dee tilted her head in question and Marion opened her mouth to speak, and then changed her mind. Dee waited.

'Let's just say I think Eva has the best protection possible.'

'Aww, thanks, Marion. That means a lot.'

Realising that Dee had misconstrued her words, Marion looked away from her. There was no way she was going to explain the complicated situation to a woman she hardly knew, even though she liked her a lot. Even if she changed her mind, she wouldn't know where to start without Dee thinking she was twenty sandwiches short of a picnic. They walked on in silence, Marion enjoying the feeling of love and security from knowing that Claire was watching over them, and Dee taking everything in around them and mentally earmarking more escape routes, should they be needed.

'Hello, my gorgeous girl,' Claire said, making some raspberry sounds that her niece found highly amusing. 'This is Trevor. He's going to look after you and do his best to keep naughty people away from you.'

Claire waited for Trevor to say something, but when he didn't, she turned to face him. His mouth was agape in a comical expression and he was looking at the woman who was with her mother and Eva.

'Trevor, what on Earth is wrong with you? You're supposed to say hello to Eva and…'

'That's her,' he said, pointing at the woman. 'That's my Dee!'

'Your Dee?'

'Dee's his little sister's name, Claire. The one who could be here with us now if he hadn't kept on saving her life. The one that my mother has told him he's got to leave alone. The one he said whose life he would stop interfering in, if the Committee gave him a chance to prove himself. Remember?'

Claire looked from Trevor to Raphael. 'But that can't be right. Why would Trevor's sister be here with Mum and Eva? That's far too much of a coincidence. I need to get to the bottom of this.'

Trying to ignore his sister and remember he had an important job to do, Trevor said hello to Eva. When he knew he had her attention he gave her his biggest smile, then did a little jig. Seeing he'd made her laugh he did the same again. She laughed out loud this time and waved her arms up and down. Taking it that she wanted more, Trevor carried on with his silliness. Then he went to say hello to the dog. Spike tilted his head from one side to the other, staring at the man who now stood in front of him, barely taller than he was. Then Trevor caressed the sweet spot between Spike's eyes.

'With our help and yours, Spike, we'll all make sure Eva stays safe.' Spike lifted his head up and closed his eyes in ecstasy.

As they stopped to look out over the lake, Dee smiled towards the dog. 'Spike seems to be enjoying the autumn sun too,' she said. 'Just look at the expression on that face.'

Marion smiled in agreement and the small group continued on their walk, Trevor still wondering why his little sister was with his charge and her grandmother.

PART TWO
Chapter 8 – Lynette and Daniel

Lynette opened her eyes and squinted as the bright sunlight found the gap in the curtains and projected itself directly onto her face. She dragged her feet out of bed and sat on the edge for a minute. Touching her face tentatively, she winced as even the gentle touch to her right cheek caused pain. Without looking in the mirror she knew her cheek was swollen, and she'd have a shiner of a black eye. But at least Paul was history now and she could concentrate on Daniel and finding a cure for him. They had an appointment that morning and it was going to go ahead, no matter how she looked or felt. This was a new stage of their lives and she tried to force some optimism into her mind – life could only get better.

She shivered as she felt something and initially hoped it was her mother looking over her. Then Lynette realised that it wasn't a pleasant feeling and put it down to the awful time she'd had with Paul the night before and the fact that her nerves were still on edge.

William, the dark-eyed demon winked at her then made his way back down the stairs.

Lynette heard shouting and it forced her into action. Grabbing her dressing gown and ignoring her pain, she rushed out of the room and hurried down the stairs. Daniel was at the sink with his Grandad standing next to him holding Daniel's hand under the running water. Blood was running from Daniel's palm.

'Daniel, what's happened? Are you all right?'

'I didn't do it, Mom,' Daniel said. His mother watched as his eyes rolled and she saw the whites.

'Quickly,' she said, knowing exactly what was about to happen. Lynette crossed to the sink in record time and caught her son before he collapsed onto the floor in one of his seizures. She sat him on a chair where his head lolled and, when she knew he was safe, looked at his hand. The bleeding had now stopped but there was a cut that looked like it might need a few stitches.

'Dad, get me the first aid box, please.'

Her father did as asked but slammed the box onto the table. 'The sooner you find somewhere else to stay, the better for all of us. Look at the state of you!'

'Don't worry, Dad,' Lynette said, trying not to cry or lose her temper, 'I'm sure Daniel will be fine and we'll be out from under your feet as soon as we can.' She looked at Beth, her father's youngest step-daughter. 'What happened?'

'Why are you looking at me? I didn't do anything wrong.'

'What happened?' Lynette repeated. She'd raised her voice and knew she was about to lose it, so again tried her best to calm down as she applied ointment to Daniel's hand and a sterile bandage.

He came around just as she'd finished and looked around the room in a panic. 'It's all right, Daniel,' she said. 'Everything's going to be all right.'

Daniel's eyes focussed above Beth and then directly on her. All the girls were used to having their own way, and although he didn't particularly like any of them, there was something about Beth that wasn't right. The main colour around her was dark orange, but it was broken and there were patches of muddy brown and black in the breaks. He didn't know the significance of these, but what he did know was that Beth was a nasty girl and, although the youngest, seemed able to control her sisters. And now there was a circle of dark grey above her, the same that preceded a violent storm, but *that* colour was also broken and interspersed with darkness. Daniel hadn't seen one like this before. Unlike the grey, this darkness shone with a strange dark light. He shivered uncontrollably before speaking.

'Beth told me she hated me, it's her fault this happened,' he said.

'I didn't, Mom. Honestly I didn't!' Beth said to her mother. 'Why would you say that, Daniel? You don't like me, and you just want to get me into trouble.' She began crying hysterically, and her mother, Nancy, put an arm around her. Beth put her head into her mother's chest and cried. Daniel was the only one who saw her sly look at him, and the cynical smile. He knew nobody would believe him.

'Like your father says, Lynette, I think the sooner you find somewhere else to live, the better.'

'Are you just going to ignore what Beth's done to Daniel?'

'You'd better tidy yourself up before Daniel's appointment this morning, Lynette. And if there's a repeat of…'

Daniel knew he was being stitched up and that they wouldn't win against his Grandad and his new family. But they needed somewhere to stay until his Mom sorted herself out. He still felt a little unsteady following his seizure, but knew he had to take charge.

'Come on, Mom,' he said. 'Let's go and get ready like Grandad says.'

He walked up the stairs, mustering as much dignity as he could, while playing out scenes in his mind of awful things happening to the horrible girl Beth, and her useless, spoilt sisters.

'Are you all right, Mom?'

'Never mind me, Daniel, I'm fine. Are you all right? Is your hand sore?'

'It is a bit, but I'll be okay.'

'We'll get the doctor to take a look later, son. What really happened this morning?'

'I was washing my hands at the sink and there was a sharp knife on the side. Beth was saying horrible things like she usually does…'

'What sort of horrible…'

'And then she pushed me,' Daniel said, interrupting his mother. 'To stop myself from falling over I went to grab onto something. I didn't see the knife and it cut my hand.'

'But why did she push you? And why was she being so horrible?'

'That's just the way she is, Mom.' Seeing how tired and bruised his mother looked, he decided not to share Beth's comments about them being white trash and her sisters joining in. The words stung more than the cut, especially when May said that his grandfather didn't want to know Daniel and his mother now that he had a proper family to love and look after.

'You do believe me, Mom, don't you?'

'Of course I believe you, Daniel! I'm so sorry I've put you in this awful situation. We'll get away from here as soon as we can. I'll find some…'

'Somewhere for us to stay, Mom?' he asked, hoping she was going to say that and not for her to find another man who would hurt her. 'Does it hurt, Mom?'

Knowing he was growing up and the truth was clear to see in the bruises on her face, Lynette nodded. 'It does a bit, Daniel. But it's made me see sense and Paul and I are finished.'

'You've said that before and.'

'I know, Daniel. But I mean it this time, honestly. I know it's hard for you to believe, but I'll show you. We'll find somewhere nice to stay and a cure for you and then we can be a happy family–you and me, son, just like everyone else.'

And we'll find a pot of gold at the end of a rainbow, Daniel thought. He wanted desperately to believe his

Mom, but also wanted to avoid yet another disappointment.

'Come on, let's get ready so we're not late for your doctor's appointment.'

*****

Lynette looked around the waiting room in the doctor's office. From the paintings on the wall to the magazines placed thoughtfully on the coffee table, everything looked stylish and, through Lynette's eyes, expensive. She'd used the last of her savings, and the money her father had reluctantly given her, to ensure Daniel could have all the tests he needed, and the best treatments to cure him when they came up with a diagnosis. After the debacle earlier that morning, she now had time to think about her father and his new wife and family for a minute. Her mom had been dead now for three years and Lynette's father had remarried six months earlier. Nancy was almost half his age, and her three daughters were a pain and spoilt little madams as far as Lynette was concerned, though she didn't realise just how spoilt, or even dangerous, Beth was. Although Nancy seemed to like her father, Lynette believed she was a gold digger and married him for his money.

Lynette had never been good with money and spent it as soon as it hit her purse. The money she inherited from her mother had been used to make memories and to partially fund her quest to find a cure for her son. Daniel had loved his holiday to Disney, and Lynette knew that unless she did the training and qualified as a beautician, she would spend the rest of her life waiting tables. She'd never be able to afford the best things in life for her son, and certainly not another holiday like that one. And before she could follow her own dream, she had to find a cure for Daniel. She frowned, remembering her father saying she should have used the money more sensibly, but the memories they both had from that wonderful holiday would stay with them for the rest of their lives, and that was certainly worth every cent!

Her relationship with her father had never been easy and he was even less interested in them both now. Lynette realised he'd only agreed to top up the money she needed for Daniel's treatment to the fifteen thousand dollars required for Daniel's medical expenses, following an argument about his abandonment. All the tests had been completed and now, here they were. The surgery nurse had taken a look at Daniel's hand, numbed it and put in a few stitches. He'd been brave and now they were waiting for the diagnosis and details of the treatment that would cure her only child.

'Daniel Brightman?' Lynette shook herself from her reverie and looked up at the nurse who smiled down at her. 'Dr Mason is ready to see Daniel. This way please.' Daniel stood up silently and followed his mother and the nurse into the doctor's surgery.

'Hello, Lynette, Daniel.' The doctor shook hands with Lynette and when he saw Daniel's right hand bandaged up, held out his other to shake.

Daniel smiled and straightened to his full height, very pleased that the doctor was treating him as a grown-up, too.

'What happened?'

'Kitchen accident,' Lynette said before Daniel could answer. 'Nurse Sue put in a few stitches and he was a brave boy, weren't you, son?' She reached over to rub his head.

'Mom!' Daniel dodged her and they all laughed.

'And you?' the doctor asked.

Even though Lynette had applied her makeup carefully, her black eye and swollen cheek were still noticeable. 'Oh, a stupid accident. You wouldn't believe me if I told you, but let's just say the post I walked into won on this occasion.'

Doctor Mason didn't believe a word of it. 'Please take a seat,' he said, with a smile.

They did as he asked, and as he studied Doctor Mason's colour, Daniel noticed there were breaks in the bluey-greens around his body. He'd seen these temporary patterns before, and he knew they wouldn't get the news they both wanted today. His smile disappeared, along with his good mood.

'Are you okay, Daniel? Are you going to have an episode?' Lynette asked.

'I'm fine, Mom,' he replied, avoiding eye contact and looking at the floor.

'You'd think he was a teenager already,' she said to the doctor, who smiled and nodded before putting on his glasses and picking up some notes.

Lynette leaned forward. 'Is it extreme Narcolepsy doctor and what's the treatment?'

'There's no easy way to say this, Lynette, so I'll come straight to the point. All the tests on Daniel have been inconclusive and the hypocretin he's been taking hasn't made the slightest bit of difference to his condition. Has he had further episodes?

'Yes he has. We haven't seen a change yet, so we need to up the dosage to make things happen and…'

'I've discussed Daniel's case and the test results with a number of experts, Lynette, and we all agree that nothing further can be done to help him. We can put you in touch with a therapist who can advise how to manage the condition so Daniel can live as normal a life as possible.'

'But there must be something medically you can do? Surely? Daniel can't live his life not knowing whether he's going to collapse at any moment! How can…'

'I'm really sorry, Lynette,' Doctor Mason said, getting up from his desk and walking around to his patient's mother. He put a hand on her arm, 'I know this is upsetting and Daniel's is an extreme condition. But many people learn to live with these unexplained conditions and live full and happy lives.'

She shook his hand off her arm. 'How can he possibly live a full and happy life when he can lose consciousness at any moment! I've paid all of this money, just for you to tell me this? And now you want me to waste more money that we don't have on a therapist?'

'Mom, please!'

They both looked at Daniel who had raised his voice. 'We knew deep down they wouldn't be able to do anything. I'll just have to be careful like I always am. It's going to be all right, Mom. Really it is.'

'Daniel's right, Lynette. And who knows, he may even grow out of the condition,' Doctor Mason said, as he noticed, not for the first time, the role reversal between mother and son whenever he told Lynette something she didn't want to hear.

'He's twelve years old for God's sake! What does he know?'

'Thanks for trying, Doctor Mason,' Daniel said, standing up. He'd heard enough and needed time to process the information, away from his mother's anger. He held out his left hand awkwardly and Doctor Mason shook it. 'I'll be outside, Mom,' he said, leaving the office and closing the door behind him.

His mother followed a few minutes later. Daniel noticed the bright yellow colour surrounding her was fading to a muddy yellow by the second. From past experience he knew this was the start of a dark mood that usually lasted for days.

'Shall we go for ice-cream, Mom?'

'Oh, Daniel,' she said, putting an arm around him and leaning her head gently onto his. A stray tear dropped onto his face and he knew he would need to be strong for his Mom.

They ate their ice-creams in silence, Lynette's favourite chocolate caramel cookie flavour and Daniel's mint choc chip. It was still early in the day and there were only a handful of other customers. Daniel wasn't in the mood to study the colours around them as he usually did when he was amongst other people, and he knew he couldn't match what he thought of as the floaty colours. They weren't always present, but sometimes he would see them hovering around some people and wondered what they meant. He shivered as he thought about the colour that appeared above Beth, knowing instinctively that it belonged to someone or something bad. His Mom looked at him.

'Are you okay, son?'

Daniel put his tongue out, stretching it as far as he could in an attempt to lick a bit of chocolate chip off his top lip. He failed and had to use his finger. 'I'm fine, Mom,' he said after licking his finger. She laughed and seemed satisfied with his answer as they carried on eating. Daniel thought about the colours again. He was learning how to match certain character traits to the colours that radiated from others, but only of the people he knew well enough. With strangers he could only look at the colours, but sometimes he watched their movements and reactions to others if the mood took him. He hoped to borrow his mother's tablet so he could do some research and see how many other people saw colours the same as he did. Again, he wondered if it was anything to do with his illness and as Daniel thought about it he felt the familiar warning signs.

As his mother asked for the bill, his head hit the table as his mind and body shut down.

'Oh my God!' said the waitress. 'Help! We need some help here!'

A couple at another table stood up and started to rush over.

'It's okay!' Lynette said. 'It's an illness. He can fall into a deep sleep any place and time.'

'Are you sure he's all right?' the man asked.

Lynette gave him a weary smile. 'Yes, and he'll be fine. But thanks anyway. We'll just stay here until he wakes up if that's okay?'

'Sure,' said the waitress, and she turned to go back to her station, shrugging her shoulders as she did so.

It was fifteen minutes before Daniel lifted his head from the table and he could see by his mother's face that she was worried.

'Sorry.'

'It's not your fault, Daniel, and you have nothing to be sorry for.'

'How long this time?'

'Fifteen minutes. Perhaps the trauma of the consultation meant your brain needed time to process?'

'I guess so, Mom. But don't worry, we're going to be just fine.'

'I know, Daniel.' She didn't know any such thing except that if conventional medicine couldn't help her son, she would have to find unconventional means.

'Come on, let's go.'

*****

Those close to Daniel knew to contact his mother if he experienced an episode, and to leave him until he woke up. Others he came into contact with were given the information, but it was frightening for those who didn't know him very well as it could be difficult to determine whether he was breathing. However, his two close friends were so used to it that they no longer felt anxious when he had an episode, and they took it in their stride. They'd cycled to his grandfather's home in the better neighbourhood, and it was these who he was now out with as his mother retreated to her bedroom with her tablet and trawled the internet for help.

Unable to find anything further through conventional medicine, Lynette Googled *alternative cures*. Halfway down the first page was a photograph of a good-looking man with black hair and shining grey eyes, named Jason Corrigan. She read the information about Jason. His biography listed him as *The Lord's Prophet*, and leader of *The Path of Jason*. It went on to say that Jason Corrigan's organisation and church were based in Arizona, and that followers could listen to his radio station, follow him on social media, and watch his podcasts or TV shows. There were claims that, with the help of God, Jason could cure the sick of heart, body, mind and soul. Lynette kept reading before shaking her head and moving on. Two hours later she had a list of people; one was a woman who could *cure all ills* by fixing chakras and there were various crystal healing therapists and homeopathic healers. She closed her laptop when Daniel returned home. Her father, his wife, and the girls had gone out to dinner without inviting Lynette and Daniel, so Lynette ordered takeaway pizzas, then they had the debate about what to watch on TV.

'The Healing Powers of Dude, Daniel?'

Daniel rolled his eyes behind his mother's back, already knowing she wanted him to be able to relate to the main character. '*Outer Banks*, Mom, please?'

He dodged his mother's hand for the second time that day when she went to ruffle his hair and they settled down together to watch the show. Looking at her son, Lynette knew she was lucky he wasn't into closing himself off and playing online games with his friends — something they'd discovered that could increase his seizures – and was even more determined to find a cure that would allow him to live as normal a life as possible.

*****

The following months were a whirlwind of activity. Lynette left her two waitressing and one cleaning jobs. Needing to get them away from her father and his new family as soon as possible, she enrolled Daniel for home schooling, and decided to travel the country in pursuit of a cure.

Daniel was excited at the prospect of visiting states he'd only seen on TV, but he soon started to miss his friends. After months of travelling and staying in cheap trailers or motels, being poked and prodded by strangers, and having to take tablets or watch crystals suspended in front of him, he was ready to go home. His mother was buying cheaper food and the treats had long since stopped, so he knew they were running out of money, though she hadn't said anything to him.

'I've had enough, Mom, I want to go home. I miss my friends, and school.'

'Do you miss your Grandad?'

'Yes.' He answered dutifully with a lie.

'But I bet you don't miss your Grandad's new family, eh Daniel?'

Daniel shivered when he remembered how cruel his Grandfather's stepdaughters were, and he looked at the scar on his hand where Beth had caused the accident with the knife. It was bad enough when her mother had refused to believe that *her little princess* was involved, but it had hurt more when his Grandad hadn't believed him either. The love that he'd felt for the man since he was young was almost non-existent now, since his grandfather's attitude to him had changed so dramatically. Daniel wanted to believe it was the influence of the woman his grandfather had married, but it wasn't. Emotionally older than his years,

103

Daniel knew that his grandfather had choices, and had chosen to bury his head in the sand and believe everything the woman and her daughters told him, rather than listen to Daniel who had never lied to him in his life. The consequences were that they were now almost like drifters, his mother was so against being anywhere near his grandfather again.

'You know it was Beth who caused this, don't you Mom?' He inspected his scar as he spoke.

'Of course, son. I know you would never lie about something like that, or anything else for that matter, and I'm still very upset that your grandfather didn't believe you. It's just us now, Daniel. But we'll be all right. I'm going to find someone who can make you better, son.'

He was glad that his Mom believed him but decided to ignore the comment about finding someone to make him better. Daniel had given up hope that would happen. He wound down the old car window, put his head out to get some air and looked at the surroundings. He reminded himself that they were in the Arizona countryside–a mountain rose from the land in the distance, with a small body of water at its base. There were patches of land that looked like they grew crops, with farmhouses and buildings scattered sparsely.

'This may be our new home, Daniel, if we like what we see tonight. You'll make lots of new friends here, there's a school, and healers. They're going to cure you.'

This time he couldn't let it go. 'Healers, Mom and a cure? But the doctor said–'

'Doctors don't know everything, Daniel. We have to trust in God and his messengers.'

They hadn't been to church on a Sunday since Daniel was a little boy, and it was as if the words had been spoken by a stranger. He'd tried to ignore the changes in his mother but now Daniel knew he had to face up to things. He needed to know how he could help her and tried to concentrate on the colours around her. They reached their destination and, as she pulled into a parking space and cut the engine, an episode hit him. Without warning, Daniel slumped down into the passenger seat.

'Oh, no, not now!' Lynette said, as she unbuckled her seatbelt and leaned over to her son. Out of habit she felt for his pulse; although it was weak, she knew that this was just another episode due to his condition. *All the more reason to do this,* Lynette thought as she tapped her fingers on the dashboard, hoping that Daniel would wake up in time for the meeting. She'd read somewhere that Jason Corrigan only gave personal presentations once every six months, and that he might be attending this one, so no way could she afford to miss it. As the minutes ticked by and Lynette chewed her nails almost down to the quick, she knew she had to do something. She opened the car door and hurried around to the passenger seat. Even knowing from experience that Daniel was like a dead weight when unconscious, she was still determined to get him into Jason's Church. She took a deep breath and opened the passenger door.

'Can we help you?' said a man's voice from behind her. Lynette was so absorbed in her own situation that she literally jumped, before turning around.

'I'm so sorry. We didn't mean to frighten you.' This time the woman spoke and, although her English was perfect, her foreign accent was stronger than her husband's.

'My son, Daniel, has an illness that can't be cured. I was hoping that…' Lynette stopped mid-flow. Not accustomed to telling her business to people she didn't know, she'd been caught off-guard and realised she was so desperate that she'd nearly told them her problems.

The woman smiled. 'We can help to take your son into the meeting hall if you like? There's a rumour that Jason himself might be here today, so we need to hurry.'

'Thank you.'

'Shall I carry him?' the man asked.

She looked from one to the other. They seemed very kind and friendly and Lynette was desperate to see Jason. 'Yes, please,' she replied. She quickly grabbed her bag and locked the car door as they made their way towards the building.

A cavalcade of cars arrived just as they approached the door, and a muscly man in a suit stopped them from entering, while another man in a suit opened the door of a limousine which nobody could see inside, due to the blacked-out windows. Lynette watched as a smallish man stepped out of the back seat. He was dressed in a pale blue suit and looked directly at the man holding Daniel, the woman with him and then Lynette. She had assumed the shiny grey of his eyes in the photograph had been enhanced by computer technology, but they looked exactly the same now, and made her feel like she was the only woman in the world.

'My, my,' he said. 'And what do we have here?'

'It's my son Daniel, Mr Corrigan. He has a sleeping illness and I've come to see if you can help.'

'Mr Corrigan's a very busy man and can't—'

'I certainly am, Oliver,' Mr Corrigan interrupted one of the suited men who had travelled in the car with him. 'But I'm never too busy to help new followers of my path. Give Daniel to me and follow me to the stage.'

The foreign man handed him over and Mr Corrigan walked in carrying Daniel, followed by

Lynette. The foreign couple also went to follow but the doorman stopped them and pointed to seats at the back of the hall.

There was uproar when the assembled congregation saw who was walking up the aisle. They stood up and cheered – then the chanting started, 'Jason, Jason, Jason…'

Jason Corrigan smiled and nodded, then said to one of his staff, 'Put two chairs on the stage for Daniel and his mother.'

The member of staff did as he was told, and by the time they had walked up the five steps onto the stage, the chairs were already in place. As the chanting continued, Jason turned to Lynette and asked, 'What's your name?'

'Lynette Brightman, and my son–'

'Your son is Daniel, yes. Sit down, Lynette.'

Totally mesmerised, and loving the attention, she took her seat, surprised at the deep rich voice coming from such a small man. Jason placed Daniel onto the chair next to Lynette's in a sitting position, and she put an arm around him so he wouldn't slump onto the floor.

'Good evening to you all,' Jason said, as the crowd continued to chant his name. He smiled and asked, 'What path are you following?'

'The Path of Jason!' everyone shouted together before breaking into cheers.

Jason lapped up the cheers from the congregation for a few seconds longer before waving his arms in a downward motion to indicate silence. As he did so, Daniel opened his eyes and sat up. His eyes darted from the stage, to the congregation, to Jason. Disorientated and frightened, he had no idea where he was.

'It's all right, son,' Jason said to him. 'You're in the presence of the Lord's Prophet and I'm going to make you better.'

Daniel tried to stand up but Lynette stopped him. 'No, Daniel. Everything's going to be all right from now on.'

Even in his confused state, Daniel could see the broken colours around the man. His main colour was bright silver, and Daniel was fascinated to see that the man's eyes were almost the same colour as his primary aura, but the silver was interspersed with black and dark grey. He hadn't seen patterns like these before and thought they were a bad sign, until the man started speaking.

'Those who have chosen *The Path* will find true enlightenment!' Jason said, holding his arms up and out. The congregation cheered again and, as they started to calm down, he looked first at Daniel and then at his adoring audience. 'The Lord has sent me a sign yet again. This boy has the sleeping illness and the Lord has chosen me to heal the boy. Stand up, Daniel.'

Jason looked at him and smiled and Daniel felt like he was the only person in the world. He also assumed he was wrong about Jason's colours and knew he would have to work harder to understand them. He smiled back and did as Jason bid. 'I will release the demons from this boy's soul and set him along *The Path of Jason*, where Daniel will find true enlightenment, happiness, and inner peace. This boy can and will be cured!'

The crowd were now in a frenzy and the cheers and chants of 'Jason' went on and on and on.

'But first, I'll send my disciples to walk amongst you. They'll tell you all about *The Path*, and details of how to join. For those specially selected members, we'll show you how you can live with us at the farm. But remember, ladies and gentlemen, numbers are limited,

108

and as much as we'd like you all to come and experience life at *The Path*, not everyone can be chosen at this time.

As his so-called disciples started mingling with the congregation, Jason turned to Lynette. 'The Lord has given me a sign and chosen you and Daniel to come to the farm.'

Lynette felt her heart swell with joy and pride, and she cried, knowing at long-last that Daniel could, and would, be cured. Overcome, she reached out and gripped Jason's hand.

'Thank you, Mr Corrigan. Thank you, thank you, thank you.'

'The Lord works his magic in many ways, Lynette. And my followers call me Jason, or the prophet. Now go and see Oliver and he'll give you the details you need. You'll have to make sacrifices while at the farm but remember why you're doing this, and all will be well.' He gave her his killer smile before jumping off the stage and bestowing his charm on others within the room.

Lynette had never met anyone like him and knew their lives would change from this day forward. She didn't yet know that the privilege of joining *The Path of Jason* would cost ten thousand dollars, and she would have to swallow her pride and call the only person who she knew would be able to loan her the money. She would also have to exaggerate the truth in order to get the money from her father. It was a small price to pay for her son to be cured and for them both to rediscover God, get to know his true prophet and feel like part of a family again. Excited about starting their new life, that night Lynette blew a little of the money she had left and they celebrated with pizza and ice-cream.

She waited until the following day before calling her father.

'Lynette! You've come to your senses then. Are you ready to admit–'

'Hello, Dad,' she interrupted him. 'How are you?'

'I'm fine, and so is my family.'

'Glad to hear it,' she said. There was an awkward pause while she waited for her father to ask how they were, but it didn't happen.

'The doctors think they've found a cure for Daniel, Dad.'

'Well that's good news. Has Daniel admitted lying about–'

'Daniel's treatment is expensive, Dad, but the specialist is confident he can cure him, and that Daniel can then live a full and happy life.'

'I see.'

'I don't think you do, Dad. We need twelve thousand dollars. It's a lot of money when we don't have it, but it's a small price to pay for a life without illness. I wouldn't ask but you're the only one who can help and my only–'

'Come home, Lynette. I miss you and Daniel, and so do Nancy and the kids. And if Daniel just admits he was wrong, we can all carry on like before.'

Lynette very much doubted that but wanted to keep her father on side. 'We belong here now, Dad,' she said. 'Daniel's met some new friends, and so have I.' Desperate to join *The Path*, she was willing to say or do just about anything to find the cash. 'I'll pay you back, honestly. Would you begrudge your only grandson, your own flesh and blood, the chance of treatment and a better life when you know that you can afford it?'

'I don't have a never-ending supply of cash, Lynette. We need to eat you know and–'

110

'I see... I guess that's it then. I have to go and give Daniel the news now. He already thinks you don't love him anymore.'

'All right, all right. But this is the absolute last! I mean it, Lynette. And you've had potential cures before that haven't worked. Whatever you think, this is the last of my savings,' he lied, 'and…' He stopped himself from telling his daughter that his wife wouldn't be happy.

'Thanks, Dad. I promise I won't ask for anymore.'

'Whether you ask or not, Lynette, the pot is empty. There's nothing left and I'm not kidding. I'll transfer seven thousand to your bank this afternoon and you can let me know how the treatment progresses. If it starts to work and you're confident the doctors can find a cure, I'll transfer the rest.

'But I need it all now Dad, they said—'

'That's my best and only offer, Lynette, take it or leave it.'

'I'll take it, thank you,' she said, wondering if they would still be able to get to the farm.

'When you get yourself a job and can take a holiday, let me know and we'll come and visit.'

Both knew that was never going to happen, but Lynette wanted to keep him sweet until the money had been transferred, so she played along. 'Daniel will love that and so will I. Bye, Dad, and thanks again.'

Lynette found the number she wanted and called Oliver, one of Jason's disciples. He said he would talk to Jason and arranged to meet her at a coffee shop near the church hall, later that day. She left Daniel in their small rented room and made her way there.

She sat down with a coffee and waited, chewing her nails as she did so. Oliver arrived ten minutes late and took a seat next to her.

111

'This is the last chance to cure Daniel,' she said, as soon as he sat next to her. 'I've seen specialists galore and tried unconventional cures. I know in my heart of hearts that Jason can help, and I've raised as much as I can, but I'm three thousand dollars short. I'm so sorry but we really need this.'

'Lots of people need lots of things, Lynette,' Oliver said, 'and Jason saves as many as he can, but he's not God almighty and he can only do so much.'

'I understand.' Her face fell. 'Are you saying he can't help us?'

Oliver smiled. 'You are one extremely lucky woman,' he said, 'Jason was unable to turn you down and he can help you.'

Lynette took her hand away from her mouth and gripped Oliver's wrist. 'Oh thank you. Thank you so much. And please thank Jason from us both. You don't know how much this means to me right now. It's like Jason's thrown us a lifeline. My son's going to be cured.' She released her grip on Oliver's wrist and wiped away a tear.

'It comes with conditions, and as you're not paying a full membership, you'll be expected to assist Jason in other ways.'

'Yes, of course. I can cook, clean, help with the paperwork if necessary–'

'Your duties have not yet been defined, but, as I say, you will be expected to help in ways that are unique to the Path.'

'I'll do whatever Jason wants.'

'He'll be happy to hear that. Read these.' He passed her a folder containing some papers. 'Your place will be ready at the farm next Wednesday.'

They said their goodbyes and Oliver left. Lynette couldn't stop smiling, knowing that at long last, their lives were taking a turn for the better.

Chapter 9 – Mission Alert

As he'd agreed with the Director, Tony was working from home; Marion had taken Eva and Spike for a walk to the local park and Tony was trying to deal with his separation anxiety.

Trigger. Call me, the text simply said, followed by the letter D. Tony stopped what he was doing and called the Director. 'No go,' the Director said, indicating to Tony that the line wasn't secure. 'I need to speak to you. Can you meet me later today?'

Tony didn't give himself time to think about it. 'Yes.'

'Okay, I'll email details. See you later.' It was short and sweet, and the Director hung up.

The email arrived a few minutes later. Tony showered, shaved and dressed in chinos and polo shirt, as opposed to the joggers and scruffy t-shirt that he wore when working from home. Dee, Marion, Eva and Spike arrived home soon after.

'Did you have a good time at the park?' he asked his daughter as he picked her up. Eva giggled into her father's chest before telling him all about their walk. He listened intently and thought he made out the words birdy and duck, but Eva might as well have been talking in Klingon for all he could understand. She yawned and her head started to nod. Tony placed her in the day cot.

'Can you postpone your class, Dee?' Tony asked. 'I've been called in.'

'Spike and I can look after Eva,' Marion said. 'You can get off to the gym.'

Dee looked at each adult in turn, wondering whether to let the situation play out or to give her opinion. Whatever happened, she wasn't leaving Eva on her own without Tony.

'Dee?'

'I can go to a class at any time. I'd rather stay here with the family while you're out. Just in–'

'I'm quite capable of looking after my own granddaughter!'

'Of course you are, Marion, and I have some online courses to do. So if it's all right with you, I'll leave you to it and do them in my room and you can call if you need me.'

Marion agreed and Tony gave Dee a big smile before looking at his daughter. 'Be a good girl for Nanna while Daddy's out,' he said, stroking her cheek. Eva was already sleeping.

Spike had waited patiently for his turn but now pawed Tony to remind him he was there. After a few minutes of making a fuss of his dog, it was time to go.

*****

Dee and Fiona were becoming firm friends and, some ten days later, the pair went out for the evening leaving Tony at home. He'd had a particularly hard training session with Jim that afternoon and nodded off during the half-time talk of the football match he was watching, with Eva asleep in his arms. Spike made a low rumbling noise which woke Tony and as he opened his eyes, he saw Spike's tail thumping gently on the floor, and that Eva was also awake. Her eyes were following something Tony couldn't see, but he sensed the presence and knew exactly who it was.

'Hello, my beautiful little Eva,' Claire said, ignoring her brother. 'It's your Auntie Claire.' Eva wriggled in Tony's arms and he placed her face-down on the settee. She looked up, at her auntie, Tony assumed, and giggled at whatever Claire was doing.

'Are you pulling faces at her or something?'

'Something like that, Tony. Isn't she getting big now?'

'She certainly is. Almost eleven months old now, Claire. She's a big girl aren't you, darling?' Now

Tony picked Eva up above him and lifted her up and down. She giggled some more.

'She's such a happy child, considering what she's already endured in her life.'

'It's been a lot easier since Dee joined our team, and we haven't had any major incidents recently.'

Claire didn't voice her opinion that something could happen at any time. 'Hmm, and I seem to have noticed a spark between you and Dee.'

'As much as you'd like to play cupid, Claire, my relationship with Dee is purely professional and there's nothing romantic between us.'

Claire didn't believe him for a second but decided to leave it and changed the subject. 'Much as I love to visit Eva and would love to chat about you and Dee, that's not the reason I'm here today. It's bad news I'm afraid… but not directly for us, Tony.'

'What's happened now?'

'The case you, Jim and Ryan are working on in Holland? Well, you know Ruben Groot couldn't stand the guilt any more and took his own life?'

'Yes, I do, and that's so sad.' Tony shook his head and looked at his daughter. 'Her mother caused so much chaos in her short life. How can I explain to Eva the sort of person she was?'

'Eva's mother was a decent person, Tony, who through no fault of her own, was targeted by evil who wanted to destroy everyone and everything in her path.'

'Including me.'

'Including those vulnerable people who didn't know any better. You weren't to know.'

'But you warned me, and I–'

'You can either put this behind you, Tony, and move on, or you can let it destroy you. Look what happened to Ruben Groot when he refused to forgive himself for his mistake.'

'It's hardly the same.'

'I know. I'm trying to demonstrate what can happen when someone can't forgive themselves. Look at Libby's Mum, too.'

Tony winced at the reminder and Claire knew she'd gone too far. 'I'm sorry to bring that up but we need you to be strong and to move on. Eva needs you to be strong. It's going to be difficult enough bringing up such a gifted child and you don't need to make it any harder.'

They both looked at Eva, who looked up at Claire and smiled, then wriggled around onto her front and held her arms out to her father. He picked her up, enveloped her in his arms and closed his eyes. Claire could see the strength of his feelings from the look on his face and gave him a moment. A few seconds later he opened his eyes. 'I think we'll put the Telly Tubbies on for you Eva,' he said, and his daughter climbed down from the settee and made herself comfortable, leaning against Spike who wasn't the least bit bothered. She was soon engrossed in the programme, so Tony and Claire carried on their conversation.

'The bad news is that Ruben's parents are finding it hard to cope and some intervention may be needed. Will you be involved in the mission if it comes to it?'

'I'm doing all of my work from home and I don't plan on travelling for a while. I don't think I could concentrate if I left Eva here with Dee and Mum, although I know they'd do everything they could to look after her; even with, um, your army of helpers.'

'That's the right decision, Tony and the sensible thing to do. And don't be afraid to talk about your feelings – that'll stop you from losing the plot and making any bad decisions in the future.'

'You're right. And whatever I may have done in the past, look how I've been rewarded.' He smiled and nodded towards Eva. 'It's not always easy, but most of the time I feel like I've won the jackpot!'

'I can see why. She is so adorable. And I can also see why you may be hiding your true feelings and might not want to start a new relationship after what happened—'

'Claire! Can we just leave the psychoanalysis please?'

'Okay, but now you know about Ruben Groot's parents, you need to ensure that your team in Holland are extra vigilant.'

'Are there forces at work here, Claire, that we know nothing about?'

'Not at the moment but I do have a bad feeling about this. It might just be the connection with Eva's mother or—'

'Or it might just be that you're trusting your instinct, which is usually spot on. I've got it, Claire and I'll inform the Director. Is this what you came to tell me?'

'Yes, and to visit my beautiful niece of course. Bye, Tony.'

Eva said something that might have been, 'Bye bye, Auntie Claire,' but Tony wasn't sure. The atmosphere changed and, knowing she'd already left, he didn't say a word. Deciding he would let Eva finish watching the programme before taking her up to bed, Tony fired up his encrypted laptop and sent an update to the Director, copying Jim and Ryan into the email.

*****

While serving his prison sentence for crimes he hadn't committed, the former bishop had put his loyal guard, aide, and now close friend, Hans, in charge of his finances. The result was that his investments had earned a steady income and they would have no major money worries for the future. He'd also received substantial compensation for his wrongful arrest and imprisonment as well as having won a case against a national newspaper who had condemned him and misreported the facts. Half of the money from the case against the newspaper had gone to a number of national children's charities, on the understanding that the donor would remain anonymous. They all agreed without hesitation. He'd returned to the small town on the outskirts of Amsterdam, determined to clear his name and had already succeeded in doing so.

Hans passed Adam Lange an old copy of *Paranormal News*, the tabloid publication that covered stories ranging from the bizarre to the surprisingly accurate appraisals of unusual, or hitherto unexplained, events and stories their readers couldn't get enough of. Someone had taken a photograph of the former bishop leaving prison and it was this that graced the cover of the publication, with the headline, 'Bad Boy Bishop Is Innocent!'

Adam rolled his eyes at Hans and shook his head before opening the publication. The story followed the headline and continued on the next page.

Before taking his own life at just 23 years old, Ruben Groot wrote a letter admitting that he'd made a false statement about being abused by the former Bishop Lange, when Groot was a ten-year-old choir boy. Groot said he was forced into the lie by Christina Jansen – the woman who has since disappeared but is thought to have been involved in the death of Andre Robertson – son of the British entrepreneur, Andrew Roberston. Ruben received psychiatric care following his third suicide attempt earlier this month, but because he could no longer live with the guilt of his part in the former Bishop's fall from grace, was determined to take his own life.

When we contacted Mr Lange and asked for his view on the whole situation, the former bishop said: "he'd pray for the soul of his accuser, and for the loved ones he'd left behind."

118

He refused to comment when questioned about Christina Jansen.

Ex-communicated from the Catholic Church after his conviction for fraud, (in which he suspects the involvement of Christina Jansen) the former bishop said: "he's determined to clear his name of this crime, but is unable to do so until the missing woman is found." When asked whether he would like to be reinstated in the church, he responded, "No thank you. I have found another pathway in which I can carry out the Lord's work." When questioned further, he refused to elaborate.

Adam put down the magazine, pondering on what had happened since.

'Penny for them?' Hans asked, and Adam shook himself out of his reverie. He reached over to the latest edition of the magazine and opened it to the page that interested him. A photograph showed the stunningly beautiful Christina Jansen, the woman singularly responsible for his ex-communication and prison sentence. It suggested how she might have illegally entered the Bishop's residence in his former diocese and used her accountancy skills to alter his ledgers, to make it look as if he had been filtering the money.

'If Ruben hadn't explained about her blackmailing him in his suicide note, do you think the police would have investigated?' Hans asked.

'It may matter to others, Hans, but not to me. I knew all along that the demon who possessed the girl was responsible, but who would have believed me? Especially after the sexual abuse allegations.'

'And if they wouldn't believe you, what were the chances of anyone believing me, or anyone else who worked for you for that matter? I'm just glad it's over now and you've been totally exonerated and received compensation – though I know it wasn't about that. As for Christina Jansen, I hope that–'

'Remember it wasn't the girl's fault, Hans. She was also an innocent victim. Hopefully her soul is now at peace.' Adam closed his eyes and prayed silently for Christina's soul. He also prayed for forgiveness for what he hoped would happen to the soul of the evil witch who had possessed the girl for the majority of her earthly life.

'And what now, Adam?' Hans asked, still finding it difficult not to address him as Your Excellency, even though Adam had insisted he wanted to be known by his first name. He had already told Hans he wanted nothing to do with the church, and that he had decided to ignore what should have been obvious and had played a part in his sentencing.

Neither needed to earn money and Adam considered this before answering. 'I will still work for the Lord, but he's yet to show me the path he wants me to take. You are free, Hans, to come and go as you wish. I don't expect you to put your life on hold, especially now that I'm a free man.'

'I've—'

'Let me finish, please. Your loyalty and friendship saw me through my worst days in that hell hole and reminded me that, however bad life was, I could always rely on you. I have no idea what direction you want your life to take, so if you want to start something new, I'm happy for you to take all of the money and go ahead.'

'Adam, for God's sake!' Hans said, kneeling in front of the man he loved and worshipped like an older brother. 'I'm going nowhere! And if you'll allow it, I'll follow whichever path God decides you should take. That's if you'll have me?'

Adam stood and leant forward to take his friend's arms. As both men stood in front of each other, Adam put his arms around Hans and enveloped him in a hug, tears falling silently down his cheeks.

120

The following day, Adam's phone pinged, indicating an incoming email. 'Good grief, it's from Fleur and Robert Groot,' he told Hans. 'They want to meet with me.'

As he responded to their email, Adam Lange had no idea that by doing so, he would soon discover the new path that his God wanted him to take.

*****

They arranged to meet Mr and Mrs Groot at their home when the couple returned from visiting Mrs Groot's mother in Eindhoven. However, when he rang the bell at the modest house, there was no answer.

Hans had a quick look through the window. 'No sign of life,' he said, and they returned home. Adam emailed the couple sporadically during the following days and weeks but eventually gave up, having received no response.

Some weeks later, Adam received an email from Mrs Groot's mother. Introducing herself as Mrs Hilda Braam, she asked if she could have his number to call him. His phone rang within minutes of him replying to the email.

'I need to talk to you, Mr Lange. My daughter and son-in-law have left the country and I would like to discuss this with you. Could I visit with you? Or, if you were able to come to me, that would be easier.'

Estimating that she was in her late eighties, Adam took her details down. 'Does tomorrow suit, Mrs Braam?'

'I'm not going anywhere Mr Lange. Anytime between 2pm and 6pm would be agreeable.' They hung up, Adam intrigued at what the visit would bring.

'I think there's more to this than meets the eye,' he said to Hans, wondering if the Lord was sending him to help the family.

If Adam or Hans expected a doddering, absentminded, elderly lady at the old people's home in

121

which she lived, they were in for a shock. The woman was dressed in a three-quarter length, smart, tweed skirt, and a pale pink buttoned up blouse, sporting a round, darker-pink coloured brooch pinned it. Her silvery grey hair was immaculate, and her blue eyes were sharp and focussed. Sitting up straight, Mrs Braam took in every detail of her visitors as a member of the staff showed them to the public room where she was waiting.

'Can I offer you gentlemen a drink?' asked the staff member.

'We'll take tea, in my room thank you, Irene,' Mrs Braam replied on their behalf. 'With some biscuits. And don't palm me off with the cheap rubbish!'

'As if I could get away with that!' the woman replied, as she headed for the door.

Hilda Braam leaned forward to pick up her sticks, then put her weight on them. It looked like she was struggling, so Hans put his arm out, about to help.

'I can manage thanks,' she said, gradually raising herself up. She started to walk slowly – her pained expression showing the stiffness of her legs – then after a few steps her expression changed and she smiled. 'Just takes a little longer to get going these days. I'm in the end room along that corridor.' She pointed with one of her sticks and they followed.

'Can you open the door please?' Hilda addressed Hans and he did as requested. She led the way, sat down on the highest chair in the room and asked the men to sit on the settee facing her, with the coffee table in the centre of the seating arrangement.

Adam looked around at the various photographs on the walls, many of Hilda's grandson, Ruben. Her eyes followed his. 'I'm sorry for what my grandson did to you.'

122

'I've forgiven him, Mrs Braam, and you have my heartfelt condolences for your loss. He will be in a better place now and–'

'Yes, yes.' She cut him short. 'I'm also heartbroken that Ruben couldn't get over the guilt of what he'd done. He was the apple of my eye, Mr Lange, although he was weak and let that evil woman manipulate him.'

'That woman is dead, Mrs Braam. She died in a fire in a building in the Scottish Highlands. A high security building that had been an institute for the criminally insane, in fact.'

'A fitting end for an evil and calculating bitch. I hope she rots in hell.' Hilda turned her head and looked out of the window, before closing her eyes and taking a deep breath.

The tea and biscuits arrived, and Adam and Hans helped themselves and waited for Mrs Braam to compose herself. When she turned back to them, she shook her head when Hans went to pick up the teapot and poured her own, all business again.

'I know you must have been devastated at losing your calling and your freedom, Mr Lange, but how do you feel now?'

It was rare for anyone except for Hans to ask after his emotional state and Adam was both surprised and touched by the question. From what he'd seen of Mrs Braam, he knew she was too astute to be hoodwinked.

'I had lots of time to think while I was in prison, and let's just say that my thoughts about Ms Jansen were neither kind, or fitting for a man of the cloth. I've now come to terms with what happened, but like you, I also hope that the soul of the evil woman is currently rotting in hell.'

'And now? Are you going to return to the church or is it too late? What are your plans?'

'I can do the Lord's work in other ways, Mrs Braam, and Hans and I are a team in this respect. But no, I don't intend to return to the church, now, or ever. Now I'm sure you haven't asked us here to discuss my career prospects…' He smiled, knowing he could be as honest with this woman as she had been with him. 'So, how can we help you?'

'My daughter, Fleur, found Ruben's body. He shot himself in the head the day after he'd set a wedding date with his fiancée, Anne. She's lovely, Mr Lange, and stood by him through everything, but it didn't do her any good. Ruben literally blew his own brains out and my daughter will never get that image out of her head.' She took a moment to compose herself before continuing. 'Fleur has teetered on the edge since it happened and so has my son-in-law, Robert. Ruben was an only child and they're lost without him.'

'I can't imagine the pain your family is going through.'

'It gets worse. They've lost their way in life and have no idea who to turn to. That's why I suggested they contact you—it might have helped knowing that you had forgiven Ruben.'

'But you had no way of knowing that I had forgiven him, Mrs Braam.'

'Gut instinct, Mr Lange. I've trusted it for nigh on eighty-seven years and it's looked after me so far.'

'My daughter and son-in-law disappeared after arranging a visit with you. It's been two months now, and all I've had is one call from Fleur. She told me they had travelled to America to be healed, and that they had *found the path*. Those were her exact words, Mr Lange, and when I asked what path that might be, she told me she loved me, that I shouldn't worry, and that she would be in touch. That was the last I heard from her. I contacted the police but as they're both adults and have left of their own accord, there's nothing they can do.'

'I'm sorry to hear this. Do you have any other family who can help you find your daughter and son-in-law?'

'There's just us now. My son died of a heart attack three years ago. If something's happened to Fleur and Robert, I...' She took a moment to compose herself again. 'I have money, Mr Lange, lots of it. I want you and Mr Boogman to find my family and bring them back. Are you up for the job and do you think you can do that?'

'The short answers are no and no. I'm not a detective and neither is Hans, but I did wonder why the Lord sent us here today.'

'You must appreciate, Mr Lange, that I have little faith left in *the Lord* after everything my family has endured. However, I have a feeling that you are the right men for this job and as I said before, I trust my instinct.'

'Hans and I need to talk about this and do our own research. Give me two days to think about it and I'll get back to you.'

Mrs Braam looked from one to the other and already knew what their answer would be. She played along though. 'Thank you both for coming to see me, and I look forward to your next visit on Wednesday.'

Feeling like they were now being dismissed, the men stood up, said their goodbyes and left the home.

*****

'They've gone to find *the path*?' said Hans, as they boarded the train for the journey home. 'Seems a strange thing to say. Why not *their* path or *their* way?' He wondered out loud.

Adam said nothing, not surprised that his current train of thought was along the same lines as that of Hans.

125

'I assume they found something specific and whatever it was—'

'Tempted them enough to make them travel all the way to America to check it out!' Hans finished for him. 'Wow, that must have been some website.'

'Or meeting. They may have arranged to meet someone and travelled after that. Come on,' Adam said, getting up.

Hans followed. 'Where are we going?'

'Back to see Mrs Braam. We need access to her daughter and son-in-law's computer, and passwords if possible. I should have thought of this earlier.'

'We're not exactly old hands at this detective work, Adam.'

They jumped off the train with seconds to spare before the doors closed and it embarked on the journey towards Amsterdam.

Mrs Braam was surprised to see them again so soon. 'We need access to your daughter's computer and any records she or her husband might have kept about appointments or meetings,' Adam explained.

'Does this mean you're going to work for me, Mr Lange?'

'We're going to try to trace your family, Mrs Braam, yes, because we need to know that they're safe and well, but that doesn't mean we're working for you.'

'How much does an ex-communicated, ex-convict priest have to live on, I wonder?'

'I have a small stipend and Hans has is very good with—'

'The more money you have, gentlemen, the more resources will be available to you. I'm worried about my family, and at my advanced age, don't know how much time and opportunity I'll have to see them again. Will you please swallow your pride or whatever it is that's holding you back, and let me employ you to find my daughter and bring her back to me safely. Please?'

'Okay, we'll do it.' This time it was Hans who spoke, to the surprise of both Adam and Mrs Braam. 'But we'll need access to their home and everything in it. We'll need five thousand euros as a down payment for expenses and will provide invoices to show how we've spent your money, but this will be an approximation. If we have to travel outside the Netherlands, we will let you know, and you'll receive a weekly written report to your email address. Adam has had enough of the media interfering in his private life and so have I, so I intend to encrypt everything I send to you and I'll write the passwords down for you. Don't let anyone else see them please. We'll start when Adam decides to visit your daughter and son-in-law's home. I take it you have the keys?'

Mrs Braam looked from one to the other, waiting for Adam's reaction. He gave his friend a wry smile, glad to know he had some input into the decision-making process, then addressed their new client. 'Do you have spare keys?' He repeated Hans' question.

'Yes.' She lifted herself out of her chair. 'I'll be a few minutes.' Mrs Braam walked slowly to the door connecting her sitting room to her bedroom, walked through it and closed it behind her. The men sat quietly. Mrs Braam was making a phone call and, while they could hear her speak, they couldn't hear the conversation. She returned a few minutes later, coinciding with the arrival of a male member of staff entering the room. She gave him a bank card, 'Thank you, Jan,' she said, and he disappeared.

Acting as if nothing unusual had happened, Mrs Braam gave Adam the keys, aware that they knew the address due to their visit after her daughter and Robert had already left. 'I haven't been there for about six months. They used to take me out on Sundays, but it's all changed since Ruben… I'm not sure where everything is kept.'

'We'll look for anything that may help us to discover more, but rest assured we'll leave their home as we found it,' Hans said.

'Is there anything else you can tell us?' Adam asked.

'You know as much as I do. I spoke about gut instinct earlier and I don't have a good feeling about this.'

'Try not to worry, Mrs Braam.' He knew it was like telling a fish not to swim. 'Might a prayer help?'

'It didn't help Ruben, Mr Lange, so no thanks. Though I do wish you Godspeed. Ah, here he is. Thanks, Jan,' she said as the man handed her an envelope, smiled and left the room without a word.

She withdrew the bank card and then handed the envelope containing the money to Adam. 'Five thousand euros agreed as the first payment. Check it if you like.'

'That won't be necessary,' Adam said, passing the envelope to Hans who put it in his man- bag.

'I look forward to hearing your progress,' she said, and for the second time that day they shook hands and left Mrs Braam staring out of the window, with not a shred of hope showing in her eyes.

Chapter 10 – The Path of Jason

It didn't take them long to find the leaflets in the home of Fleur and Robert Groot. *The Path of Jason* was written on the front in large font, and in brackets underneath, *(This way to true enlightenment).* Below the words was a logo of a blue path, along which were silhouettes of the back of a woman and child, holding hands and walking, one presumed, to their new destination.

Inside the leaflet was a photograph of a good-looking man with teeth that almost sparkled off the page, and shiny, striking grey eyes that appeared to follow the viewer wherever he or she moved in the room. Despite the stunning smile, Hans shuddered, and Adam didn't have a good feeling either. He scanned the rest of the leaflet before dropping it onto the coffee table and turning to Hans.

'It's a cult,' he said. 'I have no doubt about it. Some of these organisations prey on the weak and vulnerable, and others are simply vehicles for narcissists who convince themselves that their word is truth and try to use their numbers of believers and followers as evidence. In my opinion, nothing good comes out of following a cult.'

'Can I have a look?' Hans asked, picking up the leaflet and giving it a quick read through. He put it down and looked at Adam. 'What if I were to play devil's advocate and say that some of these organisations may just be small churches or new religions and worship God just like the more traditional religions?'

'I'm not convinced, Hans, but carry on.'

'And what if their leaders are no different to other clergy in that they're representing God here on earth?'

'But you know as well as I do that they *are* different and their leaders haven't studied or trained to

129

be able to make the most of their calling. Do you know how long it took for me to become a Bishop, Hans? Four years to study theology, and another five years in a seminary. Then, after becoming a priest, I was lucky there was a vacancy and I was promoted quicker than average. And you know how quickly that was taken away after all of my loyalty and hard work.' Adam clicked his fingers. 'Just like that, Hans. Look, I know this isn't about me, but some days I still feel the injustices of life more than others, and as much as I ask God for answers, sometimes, none are forthcoming.'

They were both silent for a few moments, Hans giving Adam the time to collect his thoughts.

'Right, forget about my rant and let's get back to the business in hand.'

'I think that grieving parents would be a prime target for recruitment to this sort of organisation,' Hans said.

'I agree. Let's find out as much as we can about them and go forward from there.'

They spent the next few weeks researching as much as they could and discovered the organisation was located in the state of Arizona. It was easy to find out information about the charismatic leader, the self-proclaimed prophet, Jason Corrigan. It was also easy to discover that *The Path of Jason* was registered as a charity so was subject to favourable tax laws. What wasn't easy was finding any other details about the membership or his followers. Adam tried another tack by pretending they wanted to join the organisation. Using false names and an email address they'd set-up specifically for this job, they made enquiries about joining the organisation. A meeting was arranged in Amsterdam, and they discovered the Path had representatives in a number of countries worldwide.

Adam and Hans waited in a coffee shop opposite Amsterdam Station. A blond-haired man, holding one of the path's leaflets, entered and Adam put up a hand and gave him a wave.

'Hello, I'm Michael,' he said, as he neared the table. 'I've come to show you the way.'

They shook hands and Michael ordered a coffee. 'The path helps the sick and needy, and souls who've lost their way in life. We spread the word of the Lord and get them back on track,' he told them.

'So you're based in Arizona. If we wanted to join we—'

'We are based in Arizona, and Jason's flock is mostly in America, but we do have small numbers throughout Western Europe, and these are growing all the time as more people hear about the good work Jason's doing. Not everyone wants to live on the farm in Arizona, some want to follow Jason and help by making small donations so we can carry out his work. Others try to find enlightenment by following Jason's online training programme and then joining one of his weekend training camps. These members often progress to the one or two-week courses, and some even move to the farm in Arizona.'

'And if we wanted to join and move straight to the farm?'

'Well then,' said Michael with a smile. 'Jason and his disciples would welcome you with open arms.' He opened his briefcase, took out some paperwork and handed a copy each to Adam and Hans. 'These are the forms I will need you to complete. The joining fee of ten thousand dollars per person covers all food, accommodation and expenses for your time at the farm, for as long as you want to live there. Now, do you have any questions?'

'It's a very big step,' said Hans. 'But we've been thinking about this for a while. If we decide we do want to join, how long would it take and what would we need to bring with us to the farm?'

'Would we be able to meet Jason before making our decision?' Adam added.

'Jason's busy doing the Lord's work and spreading the word in North America. Only last week his healing hands cured a woman who hadn't walked for ten years. It was a miracle!' Michael's face took on an expression of awe. *He actually believes Jason Corrigan is a prophet*, Adam thought, before deciding it was time to come clean. 'If we wanted to find out whether friends of ours had joined The Path, and we needed to get in touch with them, would you be able to help us?'

Michael's expression changed from one of awe from sharing the information about Jason's abilities, to one of suppressed anger. The corner of his mouth twitched, and he snatched the paperwork out of the hands of both men and put it back in his briefcase. 'The Path of Jason is a charity and a voluntary Christian organisation that carries out the Lord's work to help souls who struggle with life or have fallen on bad times. We do not judge, and we certainly do not give their details to people who use duplicity to find out information about us. Everything we do is transparent and can be found on our website, but if adults want to join and don't wish to tell their family and friends, we cannot and will not betray that trust. You will not be welcome to join us in Arizona, and have wasted my time. I expected better from a man of the cloth, but now understand why you were defrocked.'

Adam and Hans looked at each other knowingly and Michael knew instantly that losing his temper had made him lose control and that he'd shared too much information. Before Adam responded, Michael stood up and left without further ado.

'I think we need to go on a journey, Hans,' Adam said, as he watched Michael march out of the door.

132

'Do you think Mrs Braam will be happy to fund our investigation?'

'We're going whether she will or not, even if I have to cover the costs myself. This is something I need to get to the bottom of.'

'Me too.'

*****

Mrs Braam agreed without hesitation. 'Go and find my daughter and son in law, Mr Lange, and bring them back safely.'

Following some further research and preparations, two weeks later they were at Schiphol Airport, Amsterdam, waiting to board their flight.

'Please have your passports open at your photo page and your boarding passes ready for inspection.' A woman's voice came blasting out of the speakers and Adam took a deep breath, preparing himself for the flight and the adventure that was to follow. But they had to endure the journey first and neither were looking forward to it. 'It's not so much the flying,' Adam said, to no one in particular, 'it's all the faffing about at airports and being herded from one place to another.'

'And some of the miserable officials,' Hans replied, to show his friend he was listening to him. 'I swear that some of these people would have been members of the Third Reich had they been an earlier generation.'

'You can't say that, Hans, just because the customs official kept you waiting for a while.'

'And acted as if I were a serial killer, not a tourist,' Hans replied, exaggerating to make his point.

Adam resisted the urge to remind him they weren't exactly going on holiday. He wanted to lighten Hans' mood, not make it worse. He thought about the journey again and wasn't surprised that Hans was in a foul mood: a flight to JFK airport, a journey of some

133

nine hours followed by a two-hour wait, and a second flight to Phoenix. By the time they arrived at the modest hotel they'd booked into, there it would be after nine pm and their body clocks would wonder what had hit them. Although Adam hated flying, he was both excited and wary about their forthcoming investigation. Excited, as it was a new adventure that had already made him feel useful and renewed his purpose in life; wary, because he hadn't heard anything good about cults and knew these people could often resort to violence or coercion.

'Apart from not looking forward to the journey, how are you?'

'Fine,' Hans said. 'Looking forward to doing some good and getting the Groots back. New territory for me, this.'

It was good to know that Hans felt the same as he did, and Adam was hopeful they'd be successful.

They both slept fitfully on the first flight but neither felt refreshed on arrival at JFK airport in New York. The customs process was time-consuming and more serious than it needed to be.

'How long do you intend to stay?' an official asked them both.

They had rehearsed the answer, so Adam explained. 'Arizona has always looked like a beautiful place, so we plan on spending less than a month there, and if we want to extend our holiday we'll be in touch.'

'The purpose of your trip is tourism?'

They nodded, then said, 'Yes,' when prompted to do so. 'Your occupations?'

'We both took early retirement from our Civil Service jobs back in Holland,' Hans answered this time, as he found it easier to lie. 'We won a modest sum on one of those lottery tickets which helped us to retire at a relatively young age. You know, not enough that the press were interested, but enough to make a difference.'

'Thank you, Sir,' the official interrupted. 'You'll be askcd these questions again on arrival in Phoenix and will be required to provide details of where you're staying. We're busy people, so try to answer the questions without deviating. Enjoy your visit,' he added, without giving Hans a chance to comment further.

'Shall I add winding-up customs officials to your CV?' Adam asked, as they made their way to the internal flights departure terminal.

'I needed a bit of relief from this horrendous journey.'

All tickets and papers checked, and they just had time for a quick snack before boarding their next flight.

On arrival in Phoenix, Hans signed for the hire car – a pick-up truck that he'd always wanted to drive but would come in useful should they need to travel across country – and they made their way to the hotel. They drove through the small town of Haydom and then into the other side into the countryside where the *Little Blue Heron Lodge,* named for one of the rare birds that were sometimes seen at the Bird Reserve, a fifteen-minute drive from the hotel. 'So the website says,' Hans said, but neither were in the mood for conversation. It was dark, so they couldn't see any of the stunning countryside, and as both were tired, the rest of the journey was quiet. After checking-in, they made their way to their lodge, unpacked necessities only, and crashed out until the following morning.

A ray of sunshine peeped through Adam's window, throwing light on the whole room. 'What is it?' he asked, disorientated for a moment after thinking someone had entered his room and put on the light. Soon realising he was on his own, he headed for the bathroom, which was next to his room– Hans would have to walk through the living room to get there from his own bedroom.

Finishing his ablutions, he got dressed and entered the living room, where the smell of fresh coffee assailed his senses.

'Good morning, Adam. Sleep well?'

'Like a baby. And you?'

'The same,' Hans handed him a coffee. 'We can have breakfast here or in the main restaurant in the hotel.'

'Let's check out the hotel this morning. We're here for a while so we can change our minds each day if we wish.'

They stopped outside their lodge to check out the views. Green valleys led the eyes to stunning mountains way off in the distance with not a touch of snow in sight on the summits. A few properties were dotted around, and in the distance, some of the land was patch-worked. 'Most likely old farms,' said Hans. 'Not far from here used to be the hay shipping capital of the world apparently.'

'Apparently so,' Adam said, for politeness sake, but paid scant attention to his friend's knowledge of the local history as he wondered what they would find when they eventually visited The Path of Jason, apparently known by his followers as The Farm.

'We'll spend today relaxing and getting our bodies used to the new time zone and only check out a few of the surrounding areas if we feel like it,' he said. 'Then tomorrow we'll start work properly but with discretion. We don't want to be getting into trouble while we're here. But now for a hearty breakfast, I'm starving.'

'Me too.' The men smiled at each other and made their way to the main hotel building, neither aware of what would happen at the farm, or how it would impact on their lives.

136

Chapter 11 – The Farm

William had spent some time in the ether and had picked up a few lost souls on his travels, some of whom he'd delivered to his master once he'd tired of them. Now he was bored and needed excitement. He returned to earth in search of some young people whose lives he could make a misery. He hadn't had a bad life and didn't want revenge, but evil was the way he'd been born and he didn't know or want any different.

He was drawn to an area where some demons had already gathered and William's senses showed him that none were as strong as he was.

The land was fenced off and a large sign was displayed at eye-level on the large, right-hand metal gate. It showed the same words and logo as that of the brochures. On the left-hand side gate, another, not so friendly sign, read: *This way or the highway,* *TRESPASSERS WILL BE PROSECUTED.*

To reach enlightenment, new members of *The Path* had to be accepted by Jason Corrigan, the charismatic leader that many locals would have heard preaching about his organisation and his *gift*, initially as a guest on a local radio station, but more recently, on his own station, Jason C FM, and his new TV channel. Those who believed, worshipped him, and those seeking solace from life, or answers to questions they couldn't find elsewhere, were sometimes found by Jason and his followers. His network was wide and his flock comprised of people from North America, Europe and even Asia.

The long, one-story building roughly in the middle of the enclosure was split into two, almost equal, halves and had everything that Jason's flock needed to live their modest lives. Each half comprised a sleeping area, some of which was split into private sections, a large kitchen and dining area, a learning environment, a crafting and lounging area, and a contemplation room. The right-side section was occupied by adults, and that on the left, by children.

*****

The experience so far hadn't been what Daniel had expected, nor his mom if her colours were anything to go by. There were so many breaks in her aura, and what used to be bright yellow had now turned to a permanently dull and pale colour. So pale that it was sometimes difficult to distinguish as yellow. They were only allowed to see each other for an hour a day in the common room; requests for them to meet outside this hour could only be sanctioned by Jason. Sometimes at meals, they were permitted to sit together, plus during the worship or *Path Education and Teaching* meetings and sessions. Daniel noticed that the spring in his mom's step had gone, together with the hope in her eyes. *If she'd wanted to audition for a part in a zombie film, she wouldn't even have to act*, he thought sadly.

Daniel knew how she felt. Jason's promise of a cure hadn't come to fruition. On the few occasions he'd seen him since coming to the farm, he'd still been in awe of his charisma, but there was something else that worried him. Jason's colour was broken, and the bits in between were becoming muddier and muddier. He was sometimes accompanied by colours that appeared above him that gave Daniel the creeps. As bad as they were, they weren't as sinister as those that accompanied Oliver, one of Jason's disciples. These terrified Daniel and it was all he could do not to run away whenever Oliver was in the vicinity. Daniel shook himself to get rid of any thoughts of the man. He observed Jason from a distance and noticed that his expression, when he turned away from whoever he'd been talking to, was completely different to the one he showed when facing them. Daniel's feeling about Jason was worsening as each day passed. Whenever he saw him, he also had a nervous feeling in the pit of his stomach and wanted to do anything to avoid him.

Occasionally, different children were woken at night and taken to meet Jason. 'To cure us of our ills,' a new boy, Kenneth, whispered to Daniel after breakfast one morning. 'But we're not allowed to talk about it.'

'Why?'

Kenneth waited until they were walking back to their room, just the two of them. 'Don't you listen at the learnings, Daniel?' he said quietly. 'Jason uses the power of God and the energy of the universe to perform miracles. He's like a conductor for God's work. If we talk about it too much, the energy changes and weakens, and there's less chance of success. It's a small price to pay to cure the sick.'

'He hasn't cured me.'

'Your time will come, Daniel. You'll see.'

He was right. Daniel's time came that night, when everyone else was sleeping. He felt a nudge and a dull light shone in his eyes.

'What? What's happening? Who is it?'

'It's all right, son, calm down,' a man whispered, so as not to wake the others. Daniel could barely make out the shape of the man but recognised the voice as Oliver's. 'It's your turn tonight, you've been chosen.'

There was nothing he could do and, terrified, he went along with Oliver, knowing he had no choice in the matter.

'I need to get dressed.'

'It's okay, Daniel, keep on your gown but put something on your feet. You don't need your day clothes.'

Out in the fresh, night air, Daniel tried to believe that miracles really did happen and tried his

139

best to convince himself that Jason could cure him. He let his hope and optimism outweigh his gut instinct. They headed for the hut which was a good five-minute walk away from the building. Daniel's mouth was dry, and somersaults were spinning in his stomach. He was anxious and wondered how long it would take for Jason to cure him. He also wondered how it would happen and whether he would be awake or sleeping.

They arrived at the hut and Jason himself welcomed them at the door.

'Daniel. It's your turn!' he said, before turning to Oliver. 'Wait outside, we won't be too long.' Jason's smile lit up his whole face and his eyes looked at Daniel in a way the boy hadn't seen before. It made him feel uncomfortable. It was similar to the way that Paul had looked at his mother, before he was cruel to her. As Jason entered the building, Daniel hesitated, trying to look at the colours around and above him. One that was stormy grey flickered for a second but then it seemed to disappear, along with Jason's own colour, and for the first time in ages, Daniel couldn't distinguish the colours properly and he found himself opening and closing his fists. Oliver gave him a push and Daniel stumbled into the building. The door slammed shut behind him. Daniel looked around. There was nothing in the room apart from a bed which had lit candles on either side of it.

'Lie on the bed, Daniel.'

'But I don't want to…'

'Just do it, son. Everything's going to be all right and I'm going to make you better.'

Daniel did as he was told and laid on his back.

'Turn over, Daniel, and lie on your stomach,' Jason said, lifting his blue robe. He was naked underneath, and when Daniel saw the smile on his face and his erect penis, he now understood what was going

140

to happen. The shock was too much. He felt his eyes roll up into his head and he passed out.

Daniel panicked when he woke up. He opened his eyes and quickly looked around. He was back in his own bed in the room with the other children, most of whom were sleeping. Kenneth, who'd told him not to talk about miracles, was awake and looking at him. Daniel got out of his bed and crept over to Kenneth's. Kenneth now had his eyes closed, so Daniel prodded him. He could tell he was pretending to be asleep and kept prodding until Kenneth was fed up. He eventually opened his eyes.

'Who brought me back and how long have I been here?' he asked.

'Oliver. Not sure how long ago because I went back to sleep.' Watches weren't allowed at the farm, so it was sometimes difficult to tell the time between events. 'You were still out of it so I take it that Jason didn't cure you this time?'

Daniel closed his eyes and shuddered, recalling the last thing he saw before losing consciousness. His body felt fine, telling him that nothing awful had happened to him.

'What's wrong? Was it painful?'

'It was a bit scary, yes. And I hope I don't have to go again. I would rather not be cured.'

'What happened? What did he do?'

'He couldn't do anything,' Daniel said, truthfully, 'because I was so nervous that I had one of my sleeping episodes. The last thing I remember is looking at Jason, and then I was out of it.'

'Maybe next time then,' Kenneth said. 'I can't wait for my turn to be alone with Jason.'

'Kenneth, it's…' Daniel hesitated

'What?'

'Well, maybe it's not all it's cracked up to be. If I was you I wouldn't…' The door creaked open and

Daniel rushed back to his bed before he could finish the conversation, not wanting to get into trouble for being caught out of bed, and also not wanting to be selected for Jason's special treatment, ever again. As he lay with his eyes closed, he vowed to get away as soon as he could and started to formulate a plan.

The door creaked again, and Daniel saw Oliver take another boy to meet his fate.

*****

He waited until he thought everyone was sleeping the following night and shoved a towel and his other clothes in the bed so it looked like someone was in there – from a distance anyway. Daniel put on his only pair of jeans and the trainers he'd been allowed to keep, and tucked his gown into his jeans. He got his torch and his penknife from where he'd hidden them behind the wardrobe, and made his way to the door, carefully and quietly, without turning on the torch. He was out of the door and the building shortly after, and ran around to the back of it. It was the first night of work on his escape plan. He decided not to venture too far from the building and he listened carefully for any sounds, not wanting to be caught. He knew he'd be in deep trouble if he was found out. Less than an hour later, he returned to the room and got into bed, knowing that the next night he would have to try another direction.

Daniel did the same for the following two nights, but not the third as there was a rumour that somebody would see Jason on that night. As predicted, Oliver came and took a boy. It was always boys, Daniel had heard some of the girls wondering why they were never chosen. When the door closed behind Oliver and the boy, Daniel opened his eyes to see who was missing. The empty bed belonged to a boy he didn't know. Daniel lay awake, waiting for his return. The boy was brought back a few hours later and Daniel heard him crying himself back to sleep.

142

He went out again the next night and found the perimeter fence. It was some distance from the farm building and what Daniel came to think of as the torture hut. He found a place in the fence where he thought Jason's men might not look, and started cutting with his pen knife. After two nights of working on the fence, Daniel thought he'd made a big enough gap to squeeze through. He knew they were in the middle of nowhere so he decided to make it bigger so that both he and his mother could escape. Under the light of the full moon, he carried on working without having to use his torch but, for the first time since he'd been coming out at night, he heard voices. He stopped what he was doing and listened. The voices were coming from the direction which he needed to take to return to the hut.

Daniel panicked and took off in the other direction.

He ran as far and as fast as he could until his feet told him that the land was different, and he was having to avoid trees and vegetation. When his burning lungs told him he couldn't run any more, he sunk down to the ground behind a tree, fighting for his breath. The air was still and quiet and he looked around him. The full moon cast a glow on the darkness, and he couldn't see or feel anyone near or in the distance. As soon as his breathing was under control, he got to his feet and started walking. He wondered why people were out in the middle of the night, but his main concern was that he was disorientated and had no idea where he was. Trying to suppress the panic he felt at the thought of not being back in time for the wake-up call, Daniel decided to try to find the perimeter fence and work his way back from there.

The bright lights from a vehicle came from out of nowhere. Daniel scooted towards a tree and crouched down behind it. He watched as four men left the car, armed with shovels and walked a short distance from it. They started digging and Daniel watched in fascination, wondering what on earth they were up to. The penny dropped when they returned to the car and picked up a human-sized package, returned to the hole and buried it. After the car left, he hugged his knees to his chest and cried.

By the time he returned to the accommodation, the early birds had started singing but the sun hadn't yet appeared on the horizon. A few of the other children stirred as he quickly hid his knife, torch, and clothes, and jumped into bed. Daniel had too much on his mind to be able to sleep naturally. As the thoughts raced through his head, his body decided enough was enough; he felt the familiar warning signs of a seizure and, for once, welcomed the total oblivion it would bring.

What seemed like minutes later the morning call came and Daniel woke up, feeling like he hadn't slept for three weeks. Knowing he wouldn't have the opportunity to talk to his mother until the learning session after dinner, he tried to go about his day acting as if everything was the way it should be. As they walked back to the accommodation following the evening meal, Kenneth walked by Daniel's side. Even if he hadn't noticed his weaker colours, Daniel would have known something was wrong. Kenneth looked as if he had the weight of the world on his shoulders. He looked at the ground as he walked, dragging one foot in front of the other; his mouth was turned down and his eyes were red and swollen, making it obvious that he'd been crying.

'What is it?' Daniel asked quietly.

'My Uncle Ken brought me here, and now he's gone.'

'Gone?'

'Yeah. I didn't see him at breakfast, and then, before dinner, one of the disciples pulled me to one side. He said Uncle Ken left last night without telling anyone. They think he's an addict, like my parents, and couldn't be without his drugs.'

Daniel made his face hide the shock as his mind recalled the scenes from the night before. 'I'm sorry, Kenneth.'

'It doesn't seem right to me. My uncle always told me he would look after me. I don't believe he'd just up and go without saying anything. I told him that I want to leave, to go and find him, but he said my uncle would want me to stay here. How would he know that?'

'I don't know.' Daniel knew if he told Kenneth what had happened, the boy would get himself into trouble. Escape had now become even more urgent and Daniel decided that tonight was the night to do it. He planned to speak to his mother to get them both out of there. Then they could speak to the police, tell them where Kenneth's uncle was buried, and help the others to escape too. His mother had to be his top priority– they could come back for Kenneth and the others once they were safe.

'Maybe you should give it a few days to see if he comes back. If he doesn't, maybe go and look for him then,' he said.

'I wouldn't have a clue where to start and he's the only family I have. I don't have anywhere to go,' Kenneth said. Tears ran down his cheeks and he turned away and wiped them with the back of his hand. 'I need the toilet.' Kenneth said, and rushed ahead of Daniel and the other children.

The chores that evening helped to take Daniel's mind off everything that had happened within the past twenty-four hours and Daniel enjoyed the mindless drudgery of scrubbing the floor in the large bathroom area. When everything was spic and span, he cleaned himself up and made his way to the learning room where he was allowed to sit next to his mother.

There was a short period before the teachers arrived, and those present used this to chat with their loved ones. 'How was your day, Daniel?' his mother asked. To Daniel she sounded disinterested, as if she didn't want to know the answer.

'Not good, Mom.'

'I see. I think we're doing Bible study today and–'

'I need to talk to you, Mom. Please listen to me. We need to get out of here, tonight.'

'Daniel!' Lynette said, looking around to see if anyone was eavesdropping, but families were only reunited for a short time and everyone was too involved in their own business to be bothered about what others were saying or doing. Not so the staff, who kept a wary eye out for anything that may have seemed suspicious. Daniel imagined that this was a similar situation to prison visits, and he wasn't far wrong.

'But what if we get caught?' Lynette asked, chewing her nails which were already down to the quick.

'I was taken to a shed, Mom, and Jason was going to…' He tried to calm himself but shuddered at the memory and his close escape. 'Jason made me lie on a bed on my belly. He lifted his robe and… and he was about to rape me, Mom! I was terrified and had a seizure. If I hadn't, he would have–'

'Oh Daniel!' Lynette said, putting her arms around her son. 'I'm so sorry for bringing you here. If I'd have known that Jason was…' Lynette let go of Daniel and put her arms around her own waist, hugging herself. A lone tear dropped from her cheek to her thigh. She closed her eyes and swallowed.

'Has something happened?' Daniel asked.

'It's okay. It's just the payment, that's all.'

'Mom?'

'Well, because we didn't have the full amount of money, Jason said I'd have to make payment in other ways. I was prepared to work hard, but I didn't realise the payment would mean I had to–'

'Everything okay here?'

Lynette jumped up on her seat. Both mother and son had been so wrapped up in their conversation that they hadn't heard Oliver approach.

'Oh, Oliver, you made me jump!' Lynette said, forcing a smile. 'I'm so proud of my son. He's growing quickly and turning into a fine young man, despite his illness. I don't get to see enough of him. Is it possible to have extra time together? Just ten minutes every day?'

'You know the rules,' Oliver said. 'But I'll ask and let you know.' He looked at Daniel. Although the boy was annoyed, he was also terrified of Oliver and avoided eye contact with him.

'Thank you,' Lynette said, wanting Oliver to focus on her. It was obvious to anyone that Daniel was unhappy. 'I appreciate that.'

Applause interrupted their conversation as two of Jason's disciples, the teachers for the evening, entered the room. Oliver walked away, heading for the door. He lifted his radio out of his pocket as he did so, and his conversation was nothing to do with Lynette and Daniel spending extra time together.

Daniel was disappointed he hadn't had the opportunity to tell his mother about the graves and his suspicion about Kenneth's uncle. As they got up to leave, they hugged, and he kissed her on the cheek.

'Count to five hundred tonight after lights out and darkness,' he whispered. 'Then grab anything you need and I'll meet you outside, at my end of the building.'

'I'll be there,' she said.

She wasn't.

Daniel waited for what felt like ages (but was probably only a few minutes), then he waited a little while longer. He remembered the look on his mother's face when she'd said she'd be there, and knew without a doubt that something had happened.

He had to find her and help her to escape.

He made his way to the shed of torture and hid behind the nearest tree.

On this particular night, even the security lights placed strategically along the perimeter fencing were switched off. The silence was almost palpable in the dead of night

He didn't have long to wait.

The Land Cruiser's headlights on main beam lit up the area. Daniel remained out of sight and watched from a distance as one of Jason's disciples jumped out and opened the gates. The car headed towards the torture hut. As he watched, Daniel shuddered at the memory of what had happened to him in that building. He wished he hadn't told his mother, knowing that information had pushed her over the edge and Oliver might have picked up on their anxiety during their earlier conversation.

He thought back to their time on the farm and now wished he'd planned their escape sooner. They'd met three of Jason's disciples the first day of joining *The Path* and when he'd seen the colours around two of them, he knew they were the same as one of his mother's ex-boyfriends; the one who had abused her and ended up in prison for his crimes. Daniel could read most colours and knew what sort of men the two were, before they said a word. He also knew they wouldn't get any help from the third, who had colours similar to his own mother. He wondered what had happened to the man to break him before he made the decision to join *The Path*. As he'd got to know other path members during the weeks that followed, Daniel had played his own little game to discover whether the people he met matched the personalities of the colours he saw around them. It had always been fascinating to watch the colours around children change to match their current mood or feelings. But adults were different. During their one-hour socialisation sessions after the evening meal, he always checked the colours, hoping to glean some clues from them. For the most part, the colours surrounding the adults remained the same, except for those who had experienced something unusual during the day, and Daniel was beginning to learn which ones had been brought to Jason's attention. He noticed early on that when followers were told they were to meet with Jason, their colours were bright and shiny. For some, after the meetings the colours had dulled, or their natural auras were interspersed with darkness.

Daniel knew from experience that an aura mixed with darkness was never good.

He'd had a good look at the people around him before deciding to leave earlier that day. The only bright colours were surrounded a few adults, and a number of children who hadn't yet been taken for their meetings in the dark of the night. The fear of Jason trying to molest him was worse than that of being caught trying to escape. He had a fleeting thought about whether he should run to the fence where he'd made the gap and go alone, but when it came to it, Daniel knew he couldn't leave his mother on her own and berated himself for even considering it.

He stopped thinking and shivered, even though it was a warm night. If his mom had been with him, she would have said, *'Someone walk over your grave?'* as that's the sort of feeling he experienced. Looking around, Daniel couldn't see anyone else, so he ran to the building.

In the pitch darkness, a double row of lights lit up a path each side of the door to the torture shed. Daniel watched as the car door opened and men got out, along with his mother. *Where had they taken her and what have they done to her?* he asked himself. Jason was dressed in a pale blue robe and walked at the front of the small party, towards the door. He was followed by four men dressed in jeans and t-shirts, two of whom were holding his mother by each of her arms, half carrying/half dragging her towards the door. Daniel noticed blood splattered on the t-shirts of two of the followers. His mother's colour had dulled even more, and as he watched it became more and more faint.

There were colours hovering above the small group. He took a sharp intake of breath when he noticed the stormy grey aura, even in the darkness of night. Jason reached the door and nodded towards one of the men who was not holding his mother. Without saying a word, the man hurried forward to open the door, lifting one of the lamps as he did so to light the way for his leader. Another man followed suit and picked up two lamps.

Silently praying that they couldn't see him, Daniel continued to watch from behind one of the trees. He was shaking all over and gulped in as much air as he could, trying to calm his body and mind, as he watched them all enter the building. When his breathing was under control, Daniel approached the building as quietly as he could. She'd told him to run away if she didn't appear, but he was drawn to the building like a moth to a flame and couldn't help himself. Daniel ducked behind another tree as one of the men opened the door and picked up the lamps. As he did so the man looked about and Daniel feared he'd been seen. With two lamps still in each hand, the man stretched his arms above his head and yawned. It seemed an unusual thing to do while holding four

150

lamps, but all Daniel's concentration was being put into not being found and he didn't waste any further time thinking about it. The man went back into the building and now the only light was that shining through the small, dirty windows. Breathing deeply again, Daniel ran the short distance to the small building. The air was thick and silent and carried the sound of his mother's screams. There was a sharp crack, and then silence.

Trembling now, Daniel looked through the window. His mother was tied to a chair wearing only a bloody t-shirt. Jason was facing her, and as he took off his robe, the condition of his naked body showed Daniel his intention. *So he rapes women as well as children*, was his first fleeting thought, before deciding what to do next. Knowing he couldn't save her by himself, Daniel had to escape and get help for his mother.

About to move, Jason's men turned from his mother and looked directly at him. Jason turned last and smiled at Daniel in the same way he had on the night when he'd planned to invade his body. 'Deal with him. No witnesses,' Jason said.

The demons in the room had watched silently up until that moment, but now William rubbed his hands together. 'Oh goody!' he said, wondering whether to stay and watch the man empty his seed into the unwilling woman, or to join the chase. Knowing she wouldn't be his last, he decided to follow the chase.

'Daniel! Run!' his mother screamed, and she kept screaming the same words, until there was a slapping noise, followed by silence.

He took off, knowing that this time he would be running for his life.

Through the fields and avoiding as many bushes and trees as he could, Daniel ran as hard and fast as he could. The lights from the vehicle lit the area around him but he kept going. With the the perimeter fence in sight he hoped he could make it to where he'd cut the hole, then he'd have a chance of escape.

151

Running at top speed, Daniel's foot caught in the roots of a tree and he found himself suddenly flying through the air.

Above him, William clapped his hands again and watched as they got to him just feet away from the hole in the perimeter fence.

It was all too much for the boy, but he kept crawling forward even though his knee was in agony and he felt dizzy. Daniel stood up and wobbled, knowing a seizure was coming and unable to do a thing about it. The men jumped out of the vehicle and watched in fascination as Daniel's eyes rolled up into his head and he collapsed in a heap on the floor.

One of the men felt for a pulse, but found nothing.

'Out of the way,' said the one in charge. He, too, felt for a pulse but found nothing. 'Looks like Mother Nature did our job for us.'

'But I thought Jason cured him?'

The others looked at him. 'Perhaps he's had a relapse?'

The sarcasm went over his head, 'Put a bullet in him anyway, just to be sure.'

'And then we'll have the mess in the car. This way there's no evidence.' He tapped the side of his head with a finger, looking as pleased with himself as if he'd just discovered the meaning of life.

It only took one of them to lift Daniel. The man placed him on a tarpaulin in the boot and rolled it around him.

As they drove off, William decided to re-join the fun with the man and woman and headed back to the building.

They drove for fifty miles until they found what they were looking for. They dumped Daniel's body in a skip on the outskirts of a quiet neighbourhood.

Chapter 12 – Caught Out

Adam and Hans attended their first *Path of Jason* meeting and even though they'd read about his enthusiastic followers, the fervour with which the audience were whipped up, still surprised them. Jason's so-called flock shouted and screamed when they were shown recordings of his sermons, videos where he had healed the sick, or during his attendance on various Internet chat shows and podcasts. The men joined in so as not to look conspicuous. The plan was for Adam, using a pseudonym, to apply to join, then, on arrival at the farm, he would ascertain the situation with Mr and Mrs Groot, and then pass the information to Hans on the outside. Hans would then, if necessary, mount a rescue mission, or even alert the authorities, depending on Adam's findings. If Mr and Mrs Groot had made the right decision for their futures and it transpired that they were happy in the cult, they would report back to Mrs Braam and leave. It didn't occur to either of them that some of the people in authority might be also be Jason's followers, or that a certain person had returned to visit his family, from his home in Europe.

Adam approached one of the officials following their third meeting. 'I'd like to join and live at the farm,' he said.

'Welcome to the Path of Jason, brother.' The man smiled and patted him on the shoulder. 'Fill in this form and I'll pass it to Jason. Come to the meeting next week, and if Jason has a vacancy at the farm, you'll be asked to transfer the funds to cover your upkeep – a modest one-off payment – and will be given details of what to take with you, to start you on your journey to find true enlightenment. Hallelujah, and praise the Lord and Jason!'

The man leaned his head to one side, clearly expecting a response, so Adam and Hans mustered up

153

some enthusiasm. 'Hallelujah and praise The Lord and Jason!' they repeated.

Having reported the progress so far back to Mrs Braam, they spent a few days on recces of the roads in and out of the farm, being careful not to raise any suspicions while doing so. The week soon passed. It was time for the next meeting and for Adam to discover whether there was a place for him at the farm; he didn't doubt that there would be.

The atmosphere was almost fever-pitch when the congregation was informed that none other than Jason himself was to be in attendance at the meeting. 'Put your hand up if you want the Lord's Prophet to put his healing hands on you,' shouted one of his disciples. Loads of people raised their hands into the air and the man who had shouted out walked up and down the aisle, pointing at individuals seemingly at random. 'Bring these people forward,' he ordered, and those who couldn't get to the front by themselves were helped by their relatives, or the other people near them. A collective sigh of disappointment rang around the hall from those upset not to have received the chance to be healed.

'Jason will choose one of you and you will all see that miracles do indeed happen!' said one of Jason's disciples.

This was met by cheers and shouts praising Jason, and the excitement was tangible as the congregation became impatient in anticipation of seeing their hero. The organist struck up a tune and the back door opened. A man in a long blue robe, who Adam and Hans recognised as Jason, headed up the cavalcade. He was followed by four men dressed in light blue suits, the same shade as Jason's robe, and behind them were another four men, bigger and dressed in dark suits, shirts and ties. They looked around the congregation as they followed the procession up the aisle.

Adam and Hans were in a row about halfway up inside Jason's church. As soon as they saw one of the men in blue suits, their eyes widened with recognition.

'Shit,' muttered Hans, echoing Adam's exact thought.

'He might not recognise us.'

But as their eyes locked, Adam knew there was no such luck. Michael frowned at him, then swiftly changed his expression to one of impartiality. A good poker face, thought Adam, but he hadn't been quick enough and had given his initial thoughts away.

'We're busted and I think we need to get out of here,' Hans said, looking towards the door where Jason and his procession had entered. One of the men in black suits had dropped back and was guarding it. 'It seems that Jason doesn't tolerate lateness or interruptions,' Adam said. 'We'll just have to brazen it out.'

Jason bounded onto the stage and the crowd chanted his name. 'Jason, Jason,' Adam and Hans joined in, to avoid looking conspicuous.

As usual, Jason let the adoration seep into him for a while before raising his arms, signalling silence from the crowd. 'Which path do you want to find?' he asked.

'The Path of Jason!' they shouted.

'And where will that take you?'

'To true enlightenment!' The last was followed by more cheers and whooping.

Adam and Hans had stopped chanting and watched the front as Michael approached Jason. They couldn't hear what was being said, but Jason beckoned him and leant down to listen to whatever Michael was telling him. The two men started to become nervous.

Jason stood up straight and waited for the congregation to quieten down. 'It seems that not all of you here today are true believers.'

'No!'

'Oh yes! And before I lay my healing hands on a sufferer who has travelled here today in the hope of being cured, we must rid ourselves of the darkness in our light. You men,' he said, pointing in the general direction of Adam and Hans. 'You were welcomed with smiles and kindness and have chosen to repay these good people with deceit and treachery.'

The congregation weren't sure who Jason was addressing until two of the black-suited men appeared by the row where Adam and Hans were standing. The other people in the row made way for the men in suits and one grabbed Adam by his arm, none too gently.

'Hey, steady on,' he said, but the man ignored him. As he pulled him towards the end of the row, Adam was forced to endure comments of, 'Shame on you,' and, 'May you rot in hell.' The same procedure then happened with Hans, who was also subjected to abuse from the crowd.

'Oh Lord!' beseeched Jason, looking upwards with arms outstretched and palms facing upwards. 'Banish these sinners out of our midst and return them to their hotel in Haydom.'

How on earth do they know where we're staying, thought Adam, and he could see by the way Hans looked at him that he was thinking the same. They didn't have time to ponder further as they were forced to walk the gauntlet towards the door amid a torrent of abuse. Then they were pushed roughly out of the door, landing on their backsides in the road outside the building.

Now all of these lunatics know where we're staying, Adam thought, knowing that with only a few hotels in the town, it wouldn't be difficult to find them.

'Do you think a mob will come after us with pitchforks?' asked Hans.

Adam laughed at the ridiculousness of their predicament, appreciating that his friend could find humour in most situations.

He wouldn't be laughing much during the following days.

They dusted themselves down, got into the twin cab and drove the forty minutes or so back to the hotel, both contemplating their next move in their hope of contacting Fleur and Robert Groot.

After parking up and showering to get rid of the dust, Hans took some snacks out of the cupboard and put ice in two glasses. He poured whisky and a touch of water into both and placed them on the coffee table.

'Cheers,' Adam said, taking a sip. 'I need this after that humiliating experience. Now let's think about where we go from here.'

They discussed their current situation and made a list of pros and cons. The pros list was tiny.

'We need to tell Mrs Braam that the only way for us to have any possibility of getting help from the authorities is for her to report her daughter and son-in-law as missing in America.'

'Exactly,' Adam replied. 'And then I have no idea what chance we have of convincing the police to go to the farm to ask some questions.'

'It's not like we can even watch the place for the next few days, while we wait for someone from home to contact the authorities here. Did you see the way some of those people looked at us, Hans? I can't say I want to hang around here for too long.'

'Me neither. I think we need to move further away to another town and try to be as discreet as possible until we have further information.'

'Okay. I'll phone Mrs Braam. It's not a conversation I'm looking forward to.'

He put the phone on loudspeaker and Hans listened while Adam explained everything and finished up by asking. 'Have you heard from your daughter at all?'

'Nothing. And I'm more worried as each day passes. This is so out of character for Fleur, and for Robert actually. But then everything changes when you lose...' They heard her choke back a sob.

'Mrs Braam, it's—'

'I'm all right thank you, Mr Lange. I just needed a moment. So where were we? Yes, I've already been to the police. But this time I'll tell them that I believe my daughter and son-in-law have joined a cult and I haven't heard from them since. I'll tell them I think they're in danger and I won't give them any peace until they promise to get somebody out there to check.'

'Good. And you won't mention us. We don't want them to think you're—'

'I haven't lost my marbles yet, Mr Lange, and have no intention of telling anyone about your employment—not for the present, anyway. But we will see how the situation develops, and it may be that you will have to work with the authorities in order to bring Fleur and Robert home.'

'I agree,' Adam said, looking at Hans who was nodding his head. 'But for the moment we will try to find out any further local information we can about this organisation, and won't approach the police until you confirm to them that the Dutch police have contacted them. It's a shame that the man we met in Europe has returned to Arizona but—'

'You couldn't have pencilled that in, Mr Lange. What's done is done. But I look forward to hearing some positive news from you and Mr

Boogman. Now, if you'll excuse me, it's early here and I've yet to have my first coffee of the day. I'll bid you farewell and good luck.'

'Thanks, Mrs Braam.' Suitably dismissed, Adam put down the phone. It was after eleven o'clock, and he was tired, but his mind was buzzing, and he knew he wouldn't be able to sleep if he went to bed now.

'Fancy a movie before retiring?' Hans asked, seemingly reading his mind. They settled down and flicked through the channels, eventually agreeing that *The Shawshank Redemption* was the movie of choice to take their minds off their current predicament, although Hans was surprised that Adam favoured a movie where an innocent man was convicted of crimes he did not commit.

Chapter 13 - Arizona

Ryan and Jim were working with the Sunnies in Amsterdam and had discovered that Fleur and Robert Groot had now been reported as missing, presumed to have travelled to The States. The Dutch police had information on the organisation named *The Path of Jason,* and while Jim and Ryan travelled to Amsterdam to speak to Mrs Groot's mother, Tony researched all he could about the path and its leader. They discussed it during a secure video call.

'I don't like the look of it,' Tony said. 'It seems like a classic cult to me, but the only open information I've discovered sings the praises of Jason Corrigan, the man in charge. He's done the usual stuff. You know, cured terminally ill people, touched the lame so they can walk again, cured the world starvation problem, turned water into wine—you know how it goes.'

'Do people still believe this stuff?' Jim asked, but he already knew the answer.

'Yeah, and only those specially selected followers get to live on his farm where God only knows what goes on! What did you find out?'

'Mrs Braam is understandably worried about her daughter and son-in-law and she's employed the former bishop and his friend to find them and bring them back. Take a guess where they are now?'

'All roads lead to Arizona?'

'Yup, that's about it.'

'And the police?'

'They're dealing with the police in Arizona, but as the Groots left of their own free will, and they're over the age of consent, there's not a lot they can do.'

'I see, but–'

'Already happened,' Jim said.

Ryan smiled at the way each twin knew what the other was thinking but had to interject so he could keep up with the conversation. 'What were you going to say, Tony?' he asked.

'About the Dutch police asking those in Arizona to go to *The Path of Jason,* HQ or farm, to enquire about the Groots.'

'The Dutch police have already done that. The farm is out of town, about a forty-minute drive from a place called Haydom, and the police there have reported back that they found nothing unusual, and the Groots aren't there.'

'Do you believe them?'

'I don't,' said Jim. 'I think we need to investigate.'

Tony nodded. 'Ryan?'

'I'm with Jim on this. Something isn't right and we need to be there.'

'Okay. I'll speak to the Director and get things moving by the time you return.'

'How's everything else?' Ryan asked, and the twins looked at each other again and laughed.

'What?'

'Well, I would have known if something had happened,' Jim said, as if Ryan was completely stupid.

They finished the call. Tony contacted the Director, who ordered him to arrange the trip to Arizona for Jim and Ryan, and for them to fly the following day.

*****

Adam awoke early after a restless night's sleep. After showering, he opened the bathroom door to the smell of fresh coffee. Though the sun was only starting to peep over the horizon, Hans was up and in his sports kit.

'Have you been out jogging already?'

'Yes. And I don't have good news. The coffee's poured but let me show you first.'

'What's happened?'

'Nothing that can't be fixed, but we've had a warning.' Hans walked towards the door as he talked, and Adam followed him outside. He headed the short distance to the small car park behind the lodge. There were three cars in the car park but only one which had smashed front and back windows–the twin cab they'd hired. The words, *GO HOME SINNERS!* were painted on the bonnet of the car in untidy, large white letters.

'Oh, no!' Adam shook his head. 'Well there's no mistaking that warning. Was there anything in the car for them to take?'

'Nothing except the manual that came with the vehicle and I checked earlier, it's still there.'

'Okay, I'll get some photos and–'

'Already done,' Hans replied. 'I've called the police and will call the car hire company after breakfast. We might as well take our time over breakfast as we won't be going anywhere soon.'

They returned to the chalet and drank their coffee before heading to the restaurant for breakfast.

The police and the car hire company representative arrived at the same time. The car hire firm arranged a replacement vehicle, and as Adam explained what had happened the night before at the meeting, the men noticed that the former friendly demeanour of the policeman started to change.

'Sir, Mr Corrigan and his team do lots of good work for the local community, and these are good God-fearing people. Someone's making mischief here and this is not the work of Jason or of his followers.'

'But if you'd heard–'

'I don't need to hear anything further, Sir,' he interrupted Hans. 'I'll investigate this matter and we'll be in touch if we need any more information from you. In the meantime, we don't look favourably on strangers who come into our community stirring up trouble.'

'We're not–'

162

Adam stopped Hans with a look, knowing this wasn't a discussion they could win.

'We're moving out of town this morning, Deputy, and will be out of Arizona within a few weeks. We'll try our best to keep out of trouble.'

'You see that you do that. Good day, gentlemen.'

'Good day, Deputy,' they both responded.

'He didn't ask for our forwarding address,' Hans said, after they checked out of the Little Blue Heron Lodge.

'Maybe we were unfortunate and just happened to get the one Deputy who is a follower. Let's hope they're more sympathetic in the next town, otherwise our plan will be scuppered.'

'Yeah, here's hoping. Shall I keep heading in this direction until we see somewhere we like the look of? Or do you want to stop along the road and we'll Google hotels in the surrounding towns?'

'I don't know about you, Hans, but I'd like to get some distance between us and Haydom before we decide where we're going to stay. Lessen the chances of anyone finding us and of a repeat performance of last night.'

'I agree,' Hans said, putting his foot down and watching the town disappear from his rear-view mirror.

Less than an hour later, they'd driven through another town and were waiting at traffic lights on the outskirts of Williamsville. There wasn't much traffic and a garbage truck containing two skips turned left in front of them. Hans pulled out to follow when his light turned to green. A little while later, as they came out of the other end of the town, they were the only two vehicles on the road and Hans was keen to overtake the truck at the next available opportunity. Then the garbage truck driver hit what looked like a pothole in the road. The truck's suspension dropped and then

163

rebounded, which caused the vehicle to jolt. The jolt caused one of the skips in the back of the truck to open and the contents to move around.

'Look at that.' Adam pointed to what looked like a limb hanging out of one of the skips, and Hans drove closer to the truck, to get a better look.

'Oh, Lordy, Lord!' said Adam, as the arm moved and a boy climbed out of the skip. As the truck slowed down on approach to a bend, the boy climbed down the back of the truck. Hans could see what was going to happen and slowed down. The boy jumped off the truck and landed on the road in front of them, where Hans swerved and came to a stop beside him.

The boy stood up on unsteady legs and looked around him in a blind panic.

'It's all right, young man, we're not going to hurt you,' Adam said, and saw the whites of the boy's eyes as his pupils rolled up into his head before he collapsed onto the ground.

When the boy next woke up he was in the back of the car with Adam sitting next to him. He stilled his breathing and kept his eyes closed to listen to their conversation.

'Is he still out of it?' Hans asked, glancing at the back seat from his wing mirror.

'Yes, but his pulse is steady. He's filthy though, and covered in scratches and bruises. We should get him to a hospital. I'll need to call 911 and hope it's not the deputy who attended this morning. I'll ask for an ambulance at the same time.'

'No,' Daniel said out loud, opening his eyes, and looking around in a panic. Adam saw where they landed and, as Daniel reached for the door handle, he beat him to it, and stopped him from leaving the moving car.

'I'm going. You can't take me back,' he said, screwing up his face in an attempt to fight the tears.

'You're safe with us and can trust us. We won't hurt you.'

'That's what the other men said,' Daniel replied, trying to control his shaking voice. 'Until Jason…' He couldn't finish, and leaned his head forward onto the back of the passenger seat, sobs now wracking his body.

'What's your name, son,' Adam asked. He put an arm around Daniel, but the boy cowered away, so Adam quickly removed it.

'Daniel,' he whimpered. He sat up tentatively and looked at the man sitting next to him. The colour around him was a purpley-blue; one that he'd only seen once before surrounding a friend of his mother's, who used to make them cakes, look after old neighbours, and coach a youth basketball team. He thought he might be kind, but Daniel wasn't ready to trust anyone yet.

'It looks like you've been through a terrible experience, Daniel. I'm Adam, and Hans is driving.' Hans lifted a hand from the steering wheel for a second and raised it in greeting.

'You can talk to us about it or not, it's up to you, but I think you're going to need some help and medical attention, and for that to happen we're going to have to tell the police and get you to a hospital.'

'No, you can't do that! They'll take me back to Jason and The Path and something awful will happen, like it has to my mother. She might even be dead for all I know!'

He leaned forward again, but this time he banged his fists on the back of the seat. 'Jason… He was…' He squeezed his eyes shut, shook his head and swallowed, as if to rid himself of some dreadful memory. His voice was croaky, so Adam took a bottle of water out of his rucksack and gave it to him. Daniel drank like he'd spent days in a desert, only stopping to

165

catch his breath. While he did so, Adam rummaged around in the bag for the sandwiches they'd bought earlier. He passed a pack to Daniel, who said thanks and scoffed them down. Hans put on a local radio station and the chatter and music broke the silence as Daniel finished the sandwiches. He looked for somewhere to put the wrapper and Adam held out a hand.

'Thank you,' Daniel said again, then sighed. His earlier resolve to not say anything disappeared, and he began to talk. 'Their leader, Jason, was going to do something awful to my mother. He was taking his clothes off and…I thought he only liked doing it to children, but I was wrong. And then they saw me watching and my mother screamed for me to run, so I did. But then I tripped over something and had one of my episodes. The next thing I remember is waking up in that skip just now. Maybe they thought I was already dead so they didn't kill me. And some of the police have been to the farm because I've seen them talking to Jason and his disciples, and that's why I don't want you to tell the police, in case they take me back. They must be his followers or maybe he pays them or something? But I'll have to go back to try to save my mother–if they haven't…'

He stopped and looked at each of them in turn, leaving Adam and Hans wondering about the best course of action.

'Whatever we do, you need to see a doctor, Daniel.'

'As long as you promise not to tell them what happened. The doctor might be one of them, too. And you'll have to come with me. Promise? You can say you're my uncle and his friend and you're visiting from Europe. Promise?'

'I think we should call the police,' said Hans. 'It sounds like your mother is in real trouble, Daniel.'

'What day is it?' Daniel asked, and the question threw them both.

'It's Tuesday. Why?'

'Because this happened on Sunday and I must have been out of it since then. My mother will either be back with the adults or…' He gulped back a sob and couldn't finish the sentence.

'And that's why we need to contact the police, Daniel.' This time Adam tried to convince him. 'Because if something's happened to your mother, we need to find out. But first, we're going to get you some help and we won't let anyone take you from us. Okay?'

'Okay,' Daniel said, and closed his eyes.

'Let's stop at a hotel where we can get a room, check-in, get you cleaned up and then find a doctor.'

Daniel didn't respond. Another episode had taken him away. Adam put a hand around his wrist but couldn't find even a weak pulse. He put his face near to Daniel's mouth and eventually felt Daniel's breath against his cheek. Adam allowed himself to relax, knowing that Daniel was still breathing.

'He's had a terrible shock, he's frightened – and after seeing the reaction of that policeman, I can understand why he doesn't want us to go to the police. But we have to do something. Any ideas?'

'How about we make an anonymous call to the police in one of the bordering states?' Hans said.

'Good idea. Look there.' Adam pointed up the hill in the distance. 'Think that could be hotel accommodation?'

Hans took the next left and headed up the hill. As they approached, it looked like there was one main building, with other smaller buildings to the side of it. Parking out the front, they could also see more small buildings out back.

'I'll go and take a look,' Hans said, 'and I don't intend to give our real names.'

167

He entered the main building and watched as two men in front of him checked in. They weren't local either. He placed their accents as English but couldn't tell from where.

'Hello and welcome,' the man behind the reception desk said. 'Are you looking to stay here or for directions?'

'I'm looking for a room for me and my friend and our nephew,' Hans replied. 'Not sure how long we're staying yet.'

'You're from Holland?' asked one of the men who were checking-in, and Hans nodded in response, not wishing to get into conversation in case the strangers couldn't be trusted. 'I have some colleagues who work near Amsterdam. They love it there. In fact–'

'I don't mean to be rude,' Hans said. 'But I'm in a bit of a hurry. I need to check in please.'

'Sure,' said the receptionist. 'I'll be with you in just a few minutes.' Then he turned back to the two English men. 'If you could sign here… and here, Mr Sylvester,' he pointed to the forms, 'then I'll get someone to show you to your cabin.'

'Thank you,' said Jim. 'If you tell us the number and point us in the right direction, we'll make our own way there.'

The receptionist did as he'd been asked, and Jim and Ryan headed out of the hotel, leaving the Dutch man to check into his room.

'Do you think it's a coincidence that someone is here from the Netherlands and is checking-in with another man?' Ryan asked, when they were outside, out of earshot.

'No.' Jim replied, 'but he said something about a nephew too, so we might be barking up the wrong tree. Shall we find out?'

168

They checked out the cars, and sure enough, in one of them they saw a man who looked like he could match the description of the former Bishop Lange, but they would need to get closer to know for sure. Without speaking they headed in the direction of the car, noticing a boy sleeping in the back seat next to Adam. Adam watched them from the window.

'Hello, Mr Lange,' Jim said, and Adam's surprised expression gave it away straight away. 'How do you know my name?' he asked, before his brain could stop his mouth from reacting.

'We're here to help,' Ryan said. 'Who's the boy and is he all right?'

'Never mind that,' Adam said, trying to work out how he might escape from the two men if they were part of Jason's cult.

'We're from a special law-enforcement agency in the UK,' Jim lied, recognising Adam's discomfort. 'We know that a woman named Christina framed you and you were wrongly convicted of fraud, and also accused of other crimes that you didn't commit. We also know that one of your accusers has since committed suicide and that his parents might have joined *The Path of Jason*. We're here to rescue anyone who doesn't want to be in the cult, but haven't yet decided how to do it. I'm trusting you with this information and now I ask for your trust in return. Please do not share this information with anyone but your colleague, or you could put our investigation, and our lives, in danger.'

Adam visibly relaxed. 'Hans is my friend, not colleague, and it's good to know that someone is on our side. I don't think we should talk about this here, so can we meet up once we've settled into our rooms? We need to get a doctor for the boy as a matter of urgency, and without anyone knowing who he is. I'm not quite sure–'

'I'll sort that,' Ryan said, and he took his phone out of his pocket and walked away to a quiet area of the car park where his conversation wouldn't be overheard.

He returned as soon as he'd finished speaking. 'A doctor will be here within the hour,' he said. 'I've given her our room number, one-three-nine, so let me know where you are, and I'll send her over. The doctor will only ask the necessary questions and if the boy needs to be hospitalised, we can do that without the authorities finding out.'

'But how?'

'Is the boy unconscious?' Jim interrupted, and Adam explained about him flaking out, twice since they'd met earlier that day. 'Ah, here's Hans,' he added.

'Everything all right here, Adam?' Hans's posture told them all he was ready for trouble and Adam answered quickly, in Dutch.

Hans relaxed slightly so Adam explained in English. 'He knows you're on our side and are going to help us. I'll explain the rest once we're in the room.'

Hans still looked at them with suspicion, but Jim and Ryan knew they would feel exactly the same were the tables turned.

'They've arranged for a doctor to come here to see Daniel, and the authorities won't be involved.'

The men made their way to their accommodation and found that their cabins were in close proximity to each other.

Hans carried Daniel in and laid him on the bed. He came round shortly after, none the worse for wear. 'I'm starving,' he said, and both men sighed with relief in the belief that there couldn't be too much wrong with him if he was ready to eat again.

'I ordered burgers and fries when I checked us in,' Hans said. 'They should be here as soon as you're all cleaned up. Do you need a hand?'

170

'I'm nearly thirteen!' Daniel answered, and made his way into the bathroom.

'His clothes are filthy.'

'I'll find out where the nearest shop is,' Hans replied. 'If it's not far, I'll go as soon as the doctor's been and we've heard what the English men have to say.'

There was no long-term physical damage, but the doctor treated Daniel's cuts and bruises, and informed them that he would need an x-ray on his knee. She told them to contact the local hospital and also said he was dehydrated. She strapped his knee up and prescribed rest and plenty of food, water and fresh air for Daniel's physical health. They plonked him in front of the TV in the lounge area and Daniel attacked his food with gusto.

'I'm not sure about his mental health though,' the doctor said. 'He's very upset and is going to need counselling or therapy in due course. Here's my card.' She passed it to Adam. 'I can recommend someone if you need it.'

'Thank you,' Adam said, and they saw the doctor out.

Daniel finished his food and looked at the men. 'I need to go and find my mother,' he said. 'Like now!'

'It's too dangerous, Daniel. We have to let the authorities handle this.'

'But–'

'These men are beyond bad. They think you're dead, and as long as it stays that way, you're safe. If they find out you're alive and that you're going to tell the police and FBI everything you know, they'll come looking for you.'

'But my Mom! I can't just leave her.'

'We know how hard this must be for you, Daniel,' Hans said. 'But it's now our job to keep you safe until Jason and the men who work for him are all locked away. We'll find your mother. It's what she would want us to do, I'm sure.'

Daniel knew he wasn't getting anywhere with these men. He also knew they meant well but didn't really understand how he felt. 'Okay,' he said, then he shook his head and his eyelids shut, and he slumped down on the settee.

Hans rushed to the settee and caught Daniel before he fell to the floor. 'Must be another seizure,' Hans said. 'The boy must be exhausted.' He felt for his pulse. 'It's quite fast, unlike the last time, so he's alive and well.' He picked Daniel up. 'I'll put him on his bed, he'll likely sleep for a while. Then I'll go and buy him some new clothes and we can speak to Ryan and Jim and see how we're going to do this. They seem to know what they're doing.'

Adam nodded thoughtfully and waited for Hans to return to the room. 'How is he?'

'Completely out of it again.'

It's probably a blessing in disguise. When the others get here, we can discuss everything and hopefully, the FBI will be on their way shortly.'

'Okay. I won't be long,' Hans said, and left the cabin.

Less than half an hour later, Jim and Ryan arrived, and Hans returned shortly after. 'The FBI are on their way,' Jim said. 'We're meeting them two miles from the farm in an hour. While we do that, two other agents will come here to talk to you both and Daniel. Where is he?'

'Sleeping,' Hans said. 'He had another seizure and passed out. I guess it's the shock of everything and not being able to help to save his own mother.'

Jim and Ryan looked at each other. 'Show me please.' Jim said.

'Why?' Hans and Adam asked.

'Can we just see Daniel for a minute?'

Hans looked from Ryan to Jim. They suspected something but he wasn't sure of what. 'He's been through a lot and we wouldn't dream of harming him, we're here to help–' he said, getting the wrong end of the stick.

'We know that,' Ryan said. 'But the temptation to go and find his mother might be too great for Daniel to ignore.'

Jim was already up and looking around the apartment. He opened one of the bedroom doors. Nobody was in there. He did the same with the second.

'He's not here!'

'Of course he is!' Hans replied. 'I put him there myself before I went out.'

He and Adam jumped up from the settee and rushed to the bedroom. The window was wide open and Daniel was gone.

'He can't have gone far,' Hans said, looking at his watch. 'I put him here about forty minutes ago and his knee is swollen and strapped up.'

'We'll pick him up on the way. Here's my number.' Jim gave a card to Hans. 'Call me if there are any developments.'

'And here's mine…' Adam started writing down a number.

'We already have it,' Ryan said, following Jim out of the door.

Adam and Hans looked at each other, and then at the door, in disbelief, wondering what sort of organisation these two men really worked for.

*****

'He's been gone for about forty minutes and is unlikely to have hitched a ride with a stranger, given the circumstances,' Ryan said. 'And he'd want to find the quickest route. I reckon he'd go off road but stay as near to it as possible, trying not be seen. With a bad

173

knee he won't be able to move very fast and won't have gone any further than say, two miles, max.'

'I agree and probably not even that far.'

They parked on a verge a few miles into their journey and split up. Jim headed in the direction of the farm and Ryan back towards the hotel. Jim jogged steadily and after ten minutes, he convinced himself that Daniel could not have got this far. As he stopped, he saw a flash of blue up ahead that looked out of place. He remembered Daniel having a blue top on and increased his pace. Sure enough, it was the boy and he was running ahead of him. It looked as though Daniel was in pain. He favoured his uninjured leg and moved with a lopsided lolloping jog. Jim caught up easily.

'I don't think you'll be able to keep this up for very long,' he said, conversationally.

Daniel ignored him and kept going.

'The further you run, the longer it'll take us to get back to the car and drive to the farm. The FBI are on their way and I have to meet them there. Are you coming with me or would you prefer to run there?'

Daniel stopped. 'They said I couldn't go, and I have to go and help my Mom.'

'I know. And I would have said the same. You've been through too much, Daniel, and they were trying to protect you. But I don't have the time to argue with you, or to take you back, and you may be able to help the FBI if you can remember where you saw those men digging. Let's get back to the car and go to the farm. The FBI will protect you when we get there, so you won't be able to go in until it's safe. Do you understand that?'

'Yes. But I'll be able to see my Mom when they find her?'

Jim wasn't overly optimistic but didn't plan on causing Daniel any further distress. They needed to find out what had happened to his mother for sure.

'We'll speak to whoever is in charge when we get there and they'll tell us exactly what we can do. Okay?'

It seemed to satisfy Daniel and they headed back to the car, Jim calling Ryan to tell him exactly where they were so he could come and get them when he got to the car.

They arrived at the rendezvous and the FBI agents arrived less than a minute later. Daniel was goggle-eyed when he saw the team of men and women tooled up in their armoured vests with the letters FBI emblazoned on their backs and fronts, all armed with various weapons and other equipment.

Introductions made, Special Agent Fitzgerald looked at Daniel, then the adults. 'What's the kid doing here?'

'He wants to help us find his mother and he saw men digging a grave and putting a body-shaped package into it.'

'Daniel, see that van there?' the agent said, pointing to a van with a sign saying *Tasty* on the side of it. A variety of cake designs were swirled both into the letters and below them. Daniel nodded. 'You're going to travel with my agents in there and when we get to the farm, you'll stay in the van. If they have the time, one of them will ask you some questions. I want you to tell them about when you saw the men digging the grave. And when we make the farm safe, if you can remember how to find the area, that would be really helpful.'

'But I want to come with you, to find my Mom. You don't know where the buildings are and–'

'There's equipment in the van, Daniel, that will show us where the buildings are, where people are, and the best way to get in and out. I can't let you come with us until we know the area is safe, but I'll get the team in the van to show you all the equipment. Okay?'

175

Kids were usually excited by seeing what went on in the van, but Special Agent Fitzgerald understood that Daniel was too worried about his mother to show any enthusiasm. 'Let's get going,' he said, as one of the agents opened the van for Daniel and told him to get in.

Deep down, Daniel knew they were right. He also knew he had no chance of escaping from the FBI, and even if he did, the time they spent looking for him meant it would take even longer to find out about his mother. He reluctantly stepped into the van. For a few seconds his mind was taken off his mother as he looked around at the state-of-the art equipment and the three people looking from their monitors to Daniel. They all had headsets which were either on their laps or to the side of them.

'Shall I show you how this works, Daniel?' a woman said, and nodded towards a seat for him to sit down.

Satisfied that Daniel was taken care of for now, Special Agent Fitzgerald got down to business.

As they approached the farm, one of the agents in the equipment van radioed Special Agent Fitzgerald. 'Lots of heat signals boss. Looks like crowds are running away from something. Doesn't look good.'

'Roger that. Tell the teams to disembark and to be ready for action on arrival.'

Special Agent Fitzgerald sent some of his team to the gate they'd discovered at the back of the building. They'd already received their orders. 'Good luck,' he said, 'you know what to do.' He stayed at the front with some of the others, along with Jim and Ryan.

Chapter 14 – Unrest in the Ranks

It was two days after Daniel and his mother had gone missing when the Groots had garnered enough support to speak to some of Jason's disciples. As the after-dinner learning session on the Tuesday was about to start, Fleur and Robert stood up after the introductory applause ended. Robert plucked up the courage to speak.

'Before we start tonight, we need answers to some questions,' he said. The audience murmured amongst themselves. It was against the rules and they were shocked.

The two teachers looked at Oliver.

'Sit down, Mr Groot, please.'

'I won't sit down,' Robert said. 'We want to know what's happened to Lynette and Daniel, and also to Ken. We also know about two other people who went missing three weeks ago. We need some answers.'

'If you don't sit down, Mr Groot, I will come over there and make you–'

Oliver watched as Fleur nodded towards the other people in the row. Three stood up, and then all the others joined them. The people sitting behind her stood, within a minute, all but two people in the room were on their feet. Feeling left out, they sheepishly followed suit.

'Look,' Oliver said, gentling his response. 'We don't make people stay here if they don't want to. Lynette and Daniel left of their own free will and so did Frank and Betsy, three weeks ago.'

'And Ken?' Fleur asked.

'My uncle wouldn't have left without me,' Kenneth said. 'Not in a million years.'

'I'm afraid I can't answer that–'

'See,' Kenneth said, looking around the room. 'It's obvious that–'

'I can't answer that, Kenneth, because none of us know where your uncle went. He just disappeared one night.'

'He wouldn't do that. Something's wrong.'

There were rumblings around the room and Oliver discreetly pressed a button under the lectern.

'Okay. If Lynette and Daniel left of their own free will, give us their telephone numbers and let us contact them.' Robert said.

'You know Jason's policy of contact with the outside world. I can't do that.'

'But surely you wouldn't want us to think that something bad had happened to them, would you?' Fleur asked, and a few of the men began to approach the front of the room. They stopped when the door opened and Jason walked in, his face like thunder.

He looked around, waiting for them to cheer and clap. His eyes narrowed when he was met with a wall of silence and his followers could see he was trying to hold his temper.

'We want to know what's happened to Lynette and Daniel,' Robert said. 'And my Uncle Ken and the others,' Kenneth added, feeling brave.

'I am the Lord's Prophet and I don't answer to any of you!' Jason shouted at the top of his voice, then he looked upwards. 'Lord forgive them; they know not what they do.'

'You said you don't make people stay here if they don't want to,' said one of the men. 'I'm leaving.' He started walking to the front of the hall.

Jason nodded at Oliver.

178

'Are you going to let these people push you around?' William asked, not caring whether or not Oliver could hear him. *'Who's in charge here? Go on, man, don't just stand there, jolly well do something–oh goody,'* he added, as he saw what was about to happen.

The world went into slow motion. All eyes were on the man heading towards the door, so none of them saw Oliver put his hand in his jacket pocket and pull out a pistol. 'Stop!' he yelled.

The man looked around to see Oliver pointing the weapon at him. 'Don't be so stupid,' he said, turning to put his hand on the door handle. 'Anyone coming with me?'

A man behind him took a step forward, but as he did so, a shots rang out. The bullet connected with the man who had his hand on the door. His head turned to mush as he collapsed to the floor, and his blood and brain matter ran slowly down the door he'd been about to open. As the second man looked directly at him in shock, Oliver put two bullets in his chest.

Instead of containing the audience, it had the opposite effect. Pandemonium broke out as the people in the room headed for the back exit, pushing each other out of the way in their panic to get through the door first.

Oliver shot another two people and they lay injured on the floor, doing their best to keep still and pretend to be dead. As he looked for a spare magazine to reload his weapon, most of the Path's followers escaped from the building and headed towards the perimeter fence, hoping to find cover on their way.

Those who hadn't attended the learning session had heard the shots and were already heading in the direction of the perimeter fast, as fast as they could.

Jason watched as Oliver emptied the second magazine.

'How dare they disrespect you!' Oliver said, before throwing the weapon onto the ground and leaving the building. 'I'm not finished yet!'

Seeing the rage in his expression and the madness in his eyes, Jason knew he would be heading to the arsenal to collect more guns, and woe betide anyone who got in his way. He had no interest in killing his followers, or trying to stop Oliver from going on the rampage. Jason knew *The Path* was finished, and he had devised a plan for his escape if this ever happened. He left the building and got into his four-by-four. People fled from the path of the vehicle as he drove, still terrified they would be killed, he supposed. He saw two of his disciples talking to Oliver and was taken aback when Oliver punched one of them, and then got into his own car. Shortly after, more of Jason's disciples and personal staff arrived and they all watched as Oliver headed off in his car. He noticed some of his staff were heading towards the gate while others back to where their own cars were parked.

Jason left them to it. He heard the first of the sirens as he neared his own building. He stopped his car, entered his home, and ran to his plush bedroom. His safe was in plain sight in a small alcove – nobody would dare enter without his permission so he had never felt the need to hide it. He keyed in the code. A buzz signalled the safe was open and Jason took out his passport and the bags of money he stored there. He also took out his pistol and three loaded magazines. He grabbed his briefcase from under the bed and stuffed the money, bags and passport into it. He thought for a moment, then decided he was going to leave via the gate at the back of his land. There were only two keys to this gate and Jason had one of them. He removed that from the safe and put it in the front pocket of his jeans. There was no time to pack anything else and he mentally cursed his disloyal followers, Oliver, and anyone else who came to mind, for not treating the Lord's Prophet with the reverence and respect that he deserved. Oliver would go to hell, and if Jason had his way, he would play a part in that journey.

He carried the briefcase, weapon and magazines to his car, loaded one of the magazines into the pistol and put it on the passenger seat.

As he headed in the direction of the gate at the back of his land, he was surprised to hear the sirens getting louder. It took a second for him to take in the scene. Two cars with sirens blocked his exit route, so Jason had no chance of making his escape that way. An FBI agent pointed a gun in his direction, and a second called through a loud hailer for him to stop. Jason spun the car, and headed for the main exit at the front of the building. A quick check in the rear-view mirror showed him that one of the FBI vehicles had stayed at the exit, while the other was pursuing him. It wouldn't be long before the vehicle caught up, so Jason had to make a hasty decision. Changing direction again, he headed for the area where his followers were trying to escape, assuming that Oliver would return there with more firepower, intent on causing as much death and destruction as he could.

He was right. There was chaos everywhere because Oliver had stopped his car in the middle of some flat land and was shooting at the followers who were running away. Jason watched until there were no further targets for Oliver to shoot at and the man got back into his car to catch up with some of the followers who had fled. He knew he'd made the right decision when the car that followed him began chasing Oliver, along with another FBI vehicle that had come the direction of the front gate. Jason ignored further orders to stop and get out of the car. He turned the car eastwards, still heading for the front gate but via a route that would avoid Oliver and his pursuers. He heard more sirens and knew that time was running out.

Jim and Ryan had stayed in their car at the front gate, as Special Agent Fitzgerald had ordered them to do. They saw a car approach, and as it neared, recognised the driver.

'Shall we?' Jim asked, already knowing Ryan's answer as he keyed the ignition.

Jason knew he was running out of options. He turned and headed north-east with the idea of ramming the fence and escaping that way. As he continued driving, the penny finally dropped. The FBI, or cops, or whoever they were, were behind him, the reinforced fence in front of him, and even if he did manage to get off his own land, all the country's law enforcement agencies would be looking for him. There was no way to escape.

There was also no way that he, the Lord's Prophet, was going to be locked up in jail with all of the real criminals, or be subjected to the humility of a trial. He could only image how the media would crucify him, just like his Lord Jesus was crucified, but without the cross.

Jason stopped the car. Knowing what he had to do, he took a quick last breath and picked up the pistol. 'Your prophet is coming to your house, Lord. I'm coming home!'

He put the pistol in his mouth and pulled the trigger.

Jim and Ryan stopped next to the car a few seconds later. Both shuddered when they saw the unrecognisable mess that was left of Jason Corrigan's head.

*****

William watched in despair as the events at the farm unravelled. 'Oh bugger!' he said to his hangers on, straightening the jacket of his tuxedo as he did so. 'I'm

182

just going to have to find my fun elsewhere. But first, let's make sure that Jason gets the greeting he deserves.'

There was quite a welcoming committee for the self-proclaimed Lord's Prophet; bloody and scabby gnarled hands claimed Jason as soon as his soul left his body. They pulled, poked and prodded, pinched, scratched and squeezed. Then the bodies that matched the hands manifested, leaving Jason petrified with fear.

'Where are you, Lord?' he asked desperately. 'Why have you forsaken me?' Despite everything, somewhere in Jason's mind was the belief that everything he'd done was on the Lord's instructions. He firmly believed he was a good man who'd lived a good life. 'Why are you doing this to me?' he asked.

'Hello, my man,' William said. 'These chaps are about to deliver you to a lord. Unfortunately for you, it's the lord of all hell and the universe. I would love to come and smell your fear, and hear your screams, but I have other pressing matters to attend to. Until we meet again. Toodle pip.'

Jason screamed as he was pulled downwards. When he could scream no more, he began to pray.

Nobody answered.

William spoke to the small assortment of horrors and monsters who were awaiting his orders. 'Now, do you think those annoying angels will have become blasé yet? Let's see if that little girl is ready for the taking. Follow me chaps.'

They did as they were ordered as William headed back to the ether, intent on using Eva for his own sickly pleasure.

*****

Jim radioed the Ops van to tell them what he'd found and they were asked to return to the front of the enclosure which had effectively become the mission HQ. Before they left, agents had arrived to secure their part of the scene. They updated Jim and Ryan.

'We've taken out the man on the rampage. He refused to stop shooting so we had to kill him,' one of the agents said. 'We have police and agents looking for the victims and the tally so far is nine.' She shook her head. 'A tragedy. We had to kill another staff member but have caught and arrested eleven so far. Our agents and the police are still combing the area and we'll stay here until it's secure and we have everyone rounded up. Then the police will search the entire area to ensure we haven't missed anyone. The whole place is a crime scene, but the perimeter fence is secure so it's easy to control entry and exit.' They said their goodbyes and made their way back to the front of the enclosure. When they went to the van to check on Daniel, he was deep in concentration with one of the other agents, showing them on the screen where he thought the graveyard was.

'Have you found my mom?' he asked.

'Not yet, Daniel. It's chaos in there but the agents and police are working as hard and fast as they can.' Jim said.

One of the people monitoring the screens was directing the field agents to heat sources within the enclosure; the field agents would check the area and report back to let them know if they had found a person injured, or hiding. Eventually, there were no more to be found and the enclosure was declared clear.

'Can we go and find Mom now?' Daniel asked.

'We can certainly try, Daniel.' One of the agents in the van said, and then nodded towards Jim and Ryan.

Sirens wailed as ambulances and police cars arrived and entered the enclosed space.

Daniel got in the car with Jim, Ryan and another agents. They were told where the rendezvous point was for the survivors and Path followers, and were given a route there which avoided having to pass any bodies; those areas had been double cordoned-off for the forensic teams to do their work.

When they arrived, people were either sitting on the grass or standing in small groups, talking quietly amongst themselves. Some were crying and hugging their friends or family members, others were shaking heads. A few were standing, looking into the distance, in their own little worlds. Police were amongst them, along with Paramedics who had set up a field triage service, but the seriously injured had long since been blue-lighted to the nearest hospital.

'Wait here for a minute,' the agent said, as she got out of the car and went to talk to one of her colleagues.

'All of their colours are broken,' Daniel said, quietly.

Jim and Ryan shared a look.

'What do you mean, Daniel? What colours?' Jim asked.

'I see colours around everyone,' he said. 'My mom said not to talk about it and you probably think I'm crazy, but I don't really care anymore. I can sometimes tell whether people are kind, sad or just plain bad, depending on their colours. I looked it up on the Internet and they call the colours auras.'

'I see,' said Jim. 'These broken colours, what do they tell you?'

'People with broken colours means they're a bit broken too. Before my mom brought me here, her colour was a bit broken, but it was also faded. She cried a lot until she met… that… until we went to a meeting and he told her that he could cure me and stop the seizures. She wanted to believe him, we both did, and now…' Daniel lifted his arms up then dropped them to his side. 'Now look what's happened…Can we find Mom now, please?'

The agent came back to the car and they followed her to a small group. Kenneth was there, and so were Fleur and Robert Groot. They all looked like they'd been crying.

'Daniel, you're okay!' Fleur said, grabbing him into a fierce hug. She loosened her grip after a few seconds and spoke again. 'We were so worried about you and your mum. Where is she?'

'That's what I was going to ask you,' Daniel said. 'We were going to escape on… I think it was on Sunday, but I can't quite remember. Anyway, I saw Jason about to…' He looked down, trying to collect his thoughts. 'Jason and his men took my Mom to the torture shed.'

The others gave him questioning looks, so Daniel explained. 'The shed where Jason does bad things to people. Where they take children and some adults during the night.'

'Oh?'

'Didn't you know?'

'No,' Fleur said.

'Well, he took me there once and I was so frightened that I had one of my seizures, and that saved me from being… I woke up in my bed in the room and nothing had happened to me. On the night me and Mom arranged to escape, I waited but she didn't come.'

Other followers had started to listen and there was now a crowd of people, eager to hear Daniel's story.

'Then I saw car lights headed for the torture shed, so I hid behind a tree. Oliver and some other men dragged Mom into the shed and she had blood on her face and there was blood on their t-shirts. I wanted to run away, but something stopped me, and I couldn't help watching when they tied Mom up and Jason started to undress. Then he turned around and looked straight at me and Mom shouted for me to run. I was off like a hare. I knew the only way to save us was to get help. But the men followed me in a car. I nearly did it! I could see the fence and I'd made a hole in it before, big enough for both of us to escape through. Then I fell over. As they came for me I panicked and must have had a seizure again. I don't know what happened after that, but next time I woke up I was in a skip in the back of a truck. I jumped out and went to run into the woods, but two men stopped me.'

The crowd looked at Jim and Ryan with appreciation.

'No, not these two–others, also with funny accents, from Europe, I think. They brought me back to a hotel and I saw a doctor and had some food. Then I pretended to have a seizure and escaped out of the hotel bedroom window. They wouldn't let me come back, see, because they said I might not be safe. But I had to come and try to find Mom. Then these two men stopped me, and we met the Feds and I stayed in their van. But now I need to find my mom. Where is she?' Daniel's words had become faster and faster, and now he looked around. He was very agitated and started to cry.

'Where's Mom? Has anyone seen her?'

A number of people shook their heads. Others just looked away, believing the worst.

'Oh, Daniel,' Fleur said, about to take him in her arms again to comfort him, but he pulled away.

'She's gone, hasn't she?' he said. 'They killed her and buried her in that graveyard, like they did with Kenneth's uncle.'

'We don't know that,' Jim said.

'I do. I just do.' Daniel crumpled to the ground. Squeezing his knees up to his chest, with his arms around his knees and his head on his arms, he sobbed his heart out.

187

Kenneth sat down by his side so their legs were touching. He started crying along with Daniel, knowing that it made sense now why his uncle hadn't contacted him, and believing the worst.

'Let's give them some space,' Jim said, and they left Daniel and Kenneth to cry themselves out, while they took Fleur and Robert to one side and explained about the men who'd picked Daniel up when he jumped from the skip.

Robert gave Fleur a confused look. 'The man our son disgraced is here to save us?'

'Yes, along with his friend and business partner, Hans. Your mother employed them, Fleur, and if it wasn't for them, we might not have arrived here with the FBI so quickly today,' Jim said.

'My mother? And it could have been even worse than–'

'Your mother was very worried about you both. Understandably. And it's best to focus on getting back to the Netherlands, I think, when the FBI have all the information they need from you.'

'You're right. I need to contact Mum before she sees all of this on the news.'

*****

Details of the cult, and the massacre, made international news shortly after the shootings. During an initial interview with one of Jason's so-called disciples, the man gave the agents the names of all of the staff. When the head and body count was carried out, it was established that three of Jason's men had disappeared.

Daniel remembered where he'd seen the men carry the package and was able to show the authorities. It hadn't taken them long to establish that it was a burial site. The area was secured and work began the following day. As the boys suspected, the bodies of Lynette, and Kenneth's uncle Ken, had been recently

188

buried there, and they were the first to be found. Due to his involvement, the authorities were keen to protect Daniel, and agents were assigned in close protection roles.

When he heard the news Daniel's body went into shut down and he had a sudden seizure, then slept for fourteen hours following it. He was admitted to hospital and monitored.

Knowing that Adam and Hans would be focussed on helping the Groots as much as they could, Jim and Ryan spoke about Daniel.

'I think he needs some stability. We can move into a serviced apartment if the Feds allow it, and move Daniel in with us until–'

'Until what, Jim?'

'Until we speak to his grandfather, the interviews are over, and his future is decided.'

'I know Daniel seemed to form an attachment to you, Jim, but I didn't realise it was a two-way thing.'

'I feel really sorry for him, Ryan. He's lost just about everything and I won't settle until he's back with his grandfather, safe and sound.'

'You're right. But we need to speak to the Director so he can put the feelers out about the missing suspects.' Despite trying, Ryan hadn't been able to obtain any information from the FBI and they needed to get a handle on how much danger there was to Daniel.

They arranged a video call with the Director shortly after.

'How's the boy?' he asked.

Jim updated him with their news. 'He's bereft and feels all alone in the world. When I mentioned his grandfather, he said they didn't get on and the new family didn't like him. He's a clever kid and perceptive, my gut instinct is that there's a real problem there and it's not sour grapes or jealousy. Daniel doesn't want to live with them.'

'I agree with Jim,' Ryan added.

'It's all irrelevant,' the Director said, sighing. 'I have more bad news I'm afraid. Daniel's grandfather had a heart attack yesterday. He died this morning.'

'Oh no!'

'When they took a blood sample on admission yesterday, they found traces of poison in his system. It seems that somebody was trying to kill him slowly. His wife has been taken in for questioning.'

'Poor Daniel,' Ryan said. 'Now he doesn't have anyone. But he's formed an attachment to Jim, and it might help if we stayed here for a while, to give the boy some stability.'

'I agree, but you can come back, Ryan, if you wish. Unless you both want to stay? I'll leave it up to you to decide. Fiona can come out to give Daniel a bit of female company, if you like?'

'Have you bugged the apartment?' Jim asked with a chuckle, before explaining that they'd already discussed this and were going to suggest the same.

'I'd love to take the credit for this but it's down to Violet, Marion, and Fiona, of course. Janine also thinks it's a good idea, Ryan, and so does Dee.'

'Dee?'

'Yes, she's getting along with everyone swimmingly, and the women are becoming firm friends.'

'That's great to hear,' Ryan said, while Jim already knew that if there had been any problems on that score, Tony would have already told him. He didn't mention to the Director how well he thought Tony and Dee were getting along, and knew it would only be a matter of time until—

'We're going to move very quickly on this,' the Director said, interrupting Jim's train of thought.

190

After discussing the logistics, they finished the call so they could call their own families and update them.

Daniel's knee was treated and by the time he was well enough to be discharged from hospital, Fiona was on the first leg of the flight to America. Ryan had booked his own return trip to the UK.

Daniel didn't take the news of his grandfather's passing as badly as they'd expected.

'I'm really sorry to tell you this,' Jim said, 'but I have some bad news about your grandfather.'

'Is he all right? I don't want to live with him and his family. His wife and Beth, the youngest, are not nice people, their colours–'

'Daniel, I'm really sorry, but your grandfather had a heart attack.'

Daniel swallowed hard, then asked, 'Is he dead?'

'They had to operate on him, and yes, he died while they were trying to fix his heart.'

'I used to love my Grandad, but he was horrible to me and my mom and didn't want us when he had his new family. I'm sad that he's dead though–I really haven't got anyone now.' He started crying again Jim moved to sit next to him on the settee. Daniel leaned into him and Jim put his arms around the boy for whom he had developed a rather paternal feeling of sympathy.

'It's going to be all right, Daniel,' he said. 'It's heart-breaking to lose your mother and then your grandfather, but we'll get you through this.'

'How?' Daniel asked.

'I don't know, but we will.'

'Will you help me?'

'Of course.'

'Will you be like, my uncle?'

'If that's what you want, Daniel, yes.'

191

'Will you help to look after me and stop people from hurting me?'

'Of course.'

'You're just saying that to make me feel better, aren't you? You'll be like the rest of them and leave me, just like my father, Mom's boyfriends, my grandfather, and now even my mother—' He started crying again.

Jim waited until he was spent before responding. 'I don't want to leave you, Daniel, and I'm not going anywhere at the moment. My wife, Fiona, is coming to stay with us for a while and we'll look after you. But we have to return to the UK where our lives are. I'm not sure when that will happen.'

'England?'

'We live in England, yes.'

'Can I come with you?'

'We're going to talk about that when Fiona gets here tomorrow. We'll pick her up from the airport and see how we all get on together.'

Jim didn't want to give the boy false hope, but measures were already in place and he hoped that Fiona would get on with Daniel as well as he did. Time would tell. In the meantime, they had some people to say goodbye to. Having been good to him and his mother at the farm, Daniel said he wanted to be there to say goodbye to them, too.

*****

Adam and Hans met up with the Groots when the authorities had finished interviewing them and asked whether they were ready to go home. They booked flights for the four of them shortly after.

Fleur cried for all the people who had died, for her son who hadn't been able to forgive himself, and for Lynette's son, Daniel, who would now have to live his life with the trauma of what had happened, and without family to comfort him. She also cried for Kenneth, who also felt all alone in the world, and she wanted to make up for not being able to stop Ruben from taking his own life. Although returning to Holland, they had already applied to adopt Kenneth and were returning to the States within the next month after spending some time with Fleur's mother. They'd discussed it, and both Fleur and Robert would be glad to take both boys, if the authorities allowed it.

'Come with us, Daniel,' she said. 'You and Kenneth can keep each other company and we can move house so that we have plenty of room for you both. We can't replace your family, but we can give you a loving home, ensure you have everything you need and that you get a good education, to make your life as an adult easier than your childhood. You can see different doctors who might be able to help you to control the seizures. A new start might be good for you, and eventually, you'll learn to live with what's happened.'

'Thanks for the offer,' Daniel said. 'I'll never forget it. But no, thank you.'

'Are you sure?'

He nodded in reply and Fleur grabbed him for one of her body squashing hugs. When she loosened her grip, she held him at arms-length. 'If you ever need anything, Daniel, don't be afraid to contact me or Robert. Do you understand?'

He nodded.

'Promise?'

'I promise.' They had one final hug, then Robert shook his hand which made Daniel feel like a grown up.

'Look after yourself, young man, and FaceTime us from time to time to let us know how you're getting on.'

Daniel said he would and they said their goodbyes to the Groots. Fleur and Robert waited as

Adam and Hans said their goodbyes before they all got into the car, heading for the airport.

'It's been a long day,' Jim said. 'Let's get back, order some pizza and chill in front of the TV.'

'I think I'll just go straight to bed,' Daniel said.

'Can you try to eat something first?'

Instead of arguing, Daniel gave Jim a weak smile, grateful that someone still cared enough about him to make him look after himself.

Chapter 15 – Defending Eva

Dee was on the carpet playing with Eva. The little girl was attempting to place various shaped objects into their correct hole and when she did so, she was rewarded with some music and a recording of her grandmother's voice saying, 'Well done, Eva, you're so clever!' Eva clapped her hands each time she got it right. Her joy was infectious, and Dee smiled along with her. She got up to stretch and, as she walked to the window to take a look outside, she thought about Tony who was working in his study. They didn't discuss his work. He'd told her he was a Sunny, like her, but she had no idea what he was doing and had no desire to find out. She did have other desires and Dee chuckled out loud when she thought about these.

'Penny for them?'

His voice surprised her, but she didn't show it.

'I'm just checking outside to ensure all's well.'

'And what's so funny about that?'

'I was thinking about one of my former colleagues,' Dee lied. 'He was a bit of a joker you know and–'

Spike's growl which took them both by surprise. They turned towards the dog. He was looking upwards. Like synchronized swimmers they looked as one from the dog to Eva. She had stopped playing with her shapes and her eyes followed something above them that Tony and Dee couldn't see. Tony knew it wasn't his sister and the hair on his neck started to stand on end. He shivered involuntarily.

'What is it?' Eva screwed up her face and started crying at the same time as Dee asked the question.

'Something other-worldly, and not good,' Tony said.

A buzzing sound filled the air and the two adults, Eva and Spike looked around, trying to find the source of the noise.

'Surprise, surprise, little girl,' William said, hovering just above Eva to mock her. Spike was at Eva's side in a flash and he growled and barked at the horrible demon above him, to no avail. He then snapped and tried biting him, but the demon taunted the dog, until he became bored with his barking and snapping. 'You'll be barking in agony very soon, you annoying beast. I'll show you–'

Dee was the first to spot the source of the buzzing making a beeline towards Eva. 'Oh my God! It looks like a giant hornet!' She crossed the room in record time and picked up the crying toddler. 'I'll protect Eva, you get rid of it…, them,' she corrected herself as the number of hornets multiplied.

Tony had already sprung into action. As Dee left the room with Eva, Tony followed and so did Spike. 'Quick, upstairs,' he said. 'And do as I say.' He closed the door to the lounge behind him trapping the hornets in the room. They all ran up the stairs as quickly as they could. 'I want you to keep the covers over you until I've dealt with this. Okay?'

Dee lay on the bed holding Eva to her chest, while Tony covered them both from foot to head and tucked the blankets around them. They could still breathe quite comfortably, but it was already getting hot and Eva became restless.

Tony watched as more hornets appeared from nowhere, exactly like those downstairs, and as much as he waved his arms and tried to distract them, they headed for Dee and Eva on the bed. As Tony tried to swoosh and swat them, they simply flew out of his reach, or the odd one stung him. He tried not to react to the pain, not wanting to frighten Eva or Dee, and watched as the hornets attempted to land, trying their

196

best to get under the cover to attack the woman and child.

Spike was running around the bed barking and snapping, doing his best to protect his charge, when Tony felt something change. He couldn't put his finger on it and knew he shouldn't stop trying to swat the terrifying insects, but for some reason he did. He looked around the room and then back to the bed. No hornets were on it and Tony knew he hadn't got them all off. Dee and Eva were still under the covers and Eva had stopped crying.

'Are you both all right?'

'Fine, just a little hot. Have they gone?'

'No, but…'

As he answered, the hornets multiplied and a swarm dived towards the bed. Just as they reached it, it looked like they hit an invisible barrier. A barrier that reduced them to ash.

'Holy moly!' Tony said, resisting the urge to use a word that he tried to avoid in Eva's presence.

Spike made a curious noise and Tony turned towards his dog. Another swarm was diving at Spike and the same thing happened. The hornets hit an invisible force-field around the dog, and were also reduced to ashes.

'What's happening, Tony?'

'Something's protecting you. The hornets keep coming but it's like there's some sort of invisible barrier in place that's stopping them from getting too near.'

'Can we come out?'

'No! They keep coming. Just stay there. I'll let you know when it's safe. '

Before he'd finished speaking, the blanket moved and Dee and Eva were exposed down to Dee's chest.

'I said to stay as you were!'

'But I didn't move anything! I thought you did!'

Dee watched in horror as five hornets headed right for them. Before they reached the bed, they smashed into whatever had been put there to guard Eva and Dee, and were turned into ash. As the ash floated towards the floor it disappeared.

'Wow!' Dee said, then laughed. 'It's my brother Trevor! He wants to show me that he's looking out for us. Thanks, Trevor,' she said, looking upwards.

'You're welcome, little sis,' Trevor answered, although he knew she couldn't hear him, but it was good enough that she knew he had helped her, and when the last of the hornets had disappeared, he waited to ensure they were safe, then lifted the barrier. 'Good work, team,' he told the two other angels who had helped and then high-fived them both. The angels weren't used to working with one so young and enthusiastic but loved his approach to his work.

'I don't think we've quite finished yet,' one of them said, nodding to the demon behind them.

'Keep away from these people or suffer the consequences,' Trevor said, trying to exude confidence that he didn't feel.

'Well hello, little man. I nearly didn't see you there.' William replied, twisting his mouth into a sarcastic smile.

Trevor had heard it all before and it washed over him. He closed his eyes and summoned as much strength as he could in order to send the evil packing.

'You think you can hurt me?' William was incredulous and laughed out loud.

The other angels in his team, Martin and Angie, appeared at Trevor's side in seconds and Trevor tried not to look surprised as another eight angels appeared out of the ether.

William was strong and powerful, but he'd used lots of his strength on the failed attack. He was exhausted and knew if he hung around for much

198

longer, they could obliterate him. The fact that he could probably take one or two angels with him did nothing to ease the fear and panic he was trying to hide. Like most bullies, he couldn't take it when the tables were turned.

'On my command, team!' Trevor said. 'Let's make sure this demon can never attack Eva and her–'

It was too late. In a whoosh of dark matter, William had already disappeared, intent on finding other children to torture and torment. But first, he needed to recharge his batteries so he would have the strength to fight any angels who tried to scupper his plans.

Chapter 16 – Light v Dark

Four of the angels sent to assist Trevor and his team had arrived back in Cherussola after sending William packing, and explained what had happened to Eva. They also passed on the information about the cult in Arizona and details about the gifted pre-teen who could read auras.

'He's in physical danger from the escapees who were the self-styled disciples of the leader, and when he learns how to use his gift properly, will also be in danger from demons who will want to use his talents to their end.'

'Where is he now?' Gabriella asked.

'One of Claire's brothers was sent to investigate the cult, along with a colleague. The boy seems to have bonded with him and they've put him on the witness protection programme. I'm not sure whether anything's been finalised yet, but it looks like he may be fostered by someone in Claire's family. They're taking him–'

'What?' Claire interrupted.

'They're taking him to the UK by the looks of it, and he's going to live with your brother and–'

'No. I would have known!'

'Enough, Claire! We don't always know what's going on there, the same as they don't know our business.'

'But–'

'But nothing. If the boy is gifted, it would actually make good sense for him to be with your brother where we could keep an eye on him. Maybe with his gifts and Eva's we can…' Gabriella stopped talking and thought for a few moments. There was silence in the chambers as all eyes were on her.

'Raphael. You and Claire go and find out exactly what's happening. Claire, if there's a chance that your brother and his wife can look after the boy, it would be to our advantage in the long run. These two children are going to be a force to be reckoned with ,by the sounds of it, and we need them both to be nurtured and educated if they're going to help us in the fight against evil. Don't dither – and report back as soon as you can.'

Raphael knew it would be a battle to stop Claire from spending too much time with her adored niece, or finding everything out about the new boy and his circumstances, but he'd fight that one when it came to it. They did as they were ordered, and left the Chambers.

Not much later, they were travelling through the ether. Claire felt the presence first before they both saw a small group of evils. Without speaking, Raphael started to fire bolts at the lesser demons, distinguishable by their dull looking orbs. The orbs changed into their true forms of monsters and demons.

Claire noticed the evil-eyed demon. He was dressed in a tuxedo as if he were about to attend a swanky function. She fired a bolt which hit him right in the solar plexus. She saw the pained expression on his face as he absorbed the hit and waited for the cockroach transformation. Nothing happened. She'd only experienced this once before and she knew she had to centre herself and send a stronger message to the demon. Looking at Raphael as she did so, she noticed his worried expression.

She summoned up her strength and threw another bolt, initially satisfied when the evil's lower body started to change. *That's better*, she thought.

The demon gave a mock look of horror when he looked down and saw six cockroach legs starting to replace the two human ones. Then he laughed. It wasn't a pleasant sound and Claire tried to hide her frustration when there was a shimmer of dark light and human legs reappeared. She knew she had more power she would need to call on, but even so, she started to feel the first misgivings. Something wasn't right about this situation.

The demon's hands had been hanging by his side. Now he lifted his left arm above his head and pointed his index finger into the air. He then brought it down and pointed it at Claire. 'Bang,' he said, firing a dark bolt at her. Now it was Claire's turn to be horrified as her own legs started to transform to those of a cockroach, and she heard the demon laugh again.

'Raphael!'

Feeling Claire's pain and distress, it was hard for Raphael to do what he had to. It took a great deal of willpower, but he closed his eyes and prayed silently for a few seconds, knowing he needed strength and calm amongst the chaos and evil, if they were to triumph. He felt the same misgivings as Claire had and now knew they would need help; Raphael prayed and hoped it would be answered, and quickly. He opened his eyes and waggled his wings, now ready for the battle.

'Use your powers to heal yourself and to rebuff his bolts, Claire. Think of love, peace, and kindness, and pity the creature. Do not, under any circumstances, let anger, fear, and despair rule your mind and your actions.' He moved quickly to her and held her hands, doing his best to ignore the six hairy insect legs that had appeared in place of her own. 'Do you understand?'

'Yes.'

Raphael had to decide whether to use his strength to cloak Claire, which would repulse further attacks from the demon but would also lessen his powers to fight the evil, or to use all of his strength to try to beat him. He looked at his soulmate for a second. Although the alien legs were scrabbling, the expression on Claire's face had changed from fear and panic to one of serenity and Raphael hoped he was about to make the right decision.

'Concentrate on your own form first, then if you have anything left, come and help me.'

She knew how dangerous it was going to be for them both, and now it was Claire's turn to summon every ounce of willpower as her lover and hero headed towards the evil-eyed monster. Claire ignored the whooshing of bolts flying through the ether and the clang of them as they hit invisible barriers, and she concentrated. She felt the horrible insect legs scrabbling and forced her mind to picture her own legs, as she walked through a bluebell wood, holding hands with Raphael, smiling at the sound of a woodpecker and the sight of two squirrels scurrying around a tree trunk. Unsure of how much time had passed, Claire opened her eyes to find her body restored to its angelic form. The effort had taken so much from her that she now struggled to remain conscious.

She fought to keep her eyes open as she looked around, desperate to locate Raphael. Her tired eyes were drawn to the lights in the distance, and as she focussed in on them, she could see he was exchanging bolts with the evil.

A bolt from each collided in the mid space between them and cancelled each other out, so they appeared to be at an impasse. Claire approached Raphael as fast as her exhausted body would allow. Even though her mind was foggy and she felt beyond drained, the nearer she got the more obvious it was that with every bolt fired, Raphael was becoming weaker. The last collision of the opposing bolts was nearer to Raphael than it was to the evil. It was now clear to Claire that he wouldn't be able to keep going for much longer, and she knew that whatever it took, she had to find the strength to help him.

'*Focus, focus, focus,*' Claire said to herself. Now at his side, she held his hand, and it gave him a boost.

'Fire after three,' he said, and started counting.

Claire did as he asked and their bolts combined.

The evil moved closer to them, and just before it hit him, there was a loud pinging noise and their light disintegrated. He laughed loud and hard this time. 'This is so much fun,' he said, 'and I'm not in any hurry. They're coming!'

Barely with it, Raphael and Claire tried to look into the distance, listening for any changes. Within a few seconds, a smell permeated through the atmosphere. It was the stench of corruption and rotten flesh, mixed with what smelt like an overflowing sewage system. Claire gagged and Raphael shook his head, trying to rid it of the smell. The next odour was one of burning, and then they heard what sounded like horses' hooves in the distance. As the noise increased, so did the stench until it felt like the smell was now a part of them. And then the horrors came into sight. They saw an army of demons heading towards them, some in chariots, some riding alongside. Many of the demons were monsters, others were in their human form—but their animals were all the same. They were nothing like Claire had ever seen before. Four-legged with body shapes similar to horses, but they were taller, *much* taller. All had angry red eyes, two horns on their heads and scales on their backs. Had it been under other circumstances, Claire would have wondered how their riders could sit astride such animals without being ripped to shreds by their scales. Flames erupted from each rider, their chariot, and their animal.

'Is it an illusion,' Claire muttered, wondering how the flames didn't reduce them to ashes.

'We need to form a circle of love.'

Claire ignored him and simply pulled him into a hug, knowing they were about to meet the same fate as Mandy and Dylan. He couldn't see her tears but felt them like warm raindrops seeping gently into his feathers. For some bizarre reason it gave him comfort.

The army of evils pulled up behind their master and waited. William stretched his arms out in front of him and, right over left, he pulled each hand towards his body, as if he were pulling in a rope. With each pull, Claire and Raphael moved nearer to him.

Claire felt something change in Raphael and sensed he still had some fight left in him. Her spirit reacted to her soulmate's and he winked at her as she looked up to his handsome face.

'Keep your eyes on me all of the time, my beautiful angel. You need to keep reminding yourself that, whatever happens, we are going to be together forever. They can't take that away from us.'

She gave a sad smile in agreement. 'Ready?' he asked.

'Yes, my love.'

As they looked into each other's eyes, Claire felt a tingling feeling starting from her toes, running up her body through her legs, torso, and wings. When it reached her head, she was filled by a strength she hadn't known before. The feeling went from her head and shot down her left arm. They loosened the hug so that they were now standing at an angle to each other, still looking into each other's eyes and still holding hands, but Claire's right hand and Raphael's left were down by their sides.

As William continued pulling them towards him using an invisible force, Raphael and Claire lifted their locked hands and fired. The first line of demons behind William turned to ash. The evils stopped moving and screams and growls came from the other creatures behind William.

'Stand your ground!' he screamed at the top of his voice, knowing they had the power to defeat the angels, but only if they worked together.

While William took time trying to control the demons, his lock on Raphael and Claire had loosened. Knowing they weren't strong enough to defeat the dark-eyed demon, when they fired for the second time, they aimed at the weaker monsters three rows behind their master, aiming to cause havoc in their ranks. Their bolt achieved the same result and now the unrest amongst the demons was palpable.

Claire and Raphael watched as a few of the braver monsters tested William by poking and prodding him. He struck the first so hard that the monster was flung, screaming, into the ether. The second was a grotesque hybrid of human and cockroach. The angels knew that someone had tried to ensnare him before to send him to the cave, but the demon had escaped. He wiggled his cockroach legs as he spoke to the legion of demons.

'If we follow William, we either get turned to ashes by the angels, or sent back to hell after we help him win the fight. But if William isn't around to report back to our master, that gives us another choice. We could escape and be free for ages, perhaps even for ever if we're clever enough.' There was no mistaking his message and the unrest in the crowd took the focus off Claire and Raphael for a few seconds.

The hybrid threw a bolt at William, and then, weaving and dodging, he moved away out of William's reach. Although the bolt had little effect and bounced off their leader, the others knew that with a combined effort they had a chance of causing him some damage.

'Don't be stupid!' William screamed. 'We can beat them and rule the ether. We can cause all sorts of havoc then, and have fun destroying the angels. We can claim all souls coming through. We can even go to earth and cause havoc–arrrghhhh!' He screamed as a number of bolts combined in mid-air and then hit him on his right arm. The black mass stripped away part of his jacket, and William smelt his flesh burning. He patted his arm with his left hand to put the fire out, burning his hand as he did so.

One of the demons giggled with glee until William looked at him and threw a bolt in anger. The demon was no more.

'Who's next?' he asked, firing a few more bolts for good measure, convincing himself their fear of him would bring them back into line. Two demons disintegrated instantly, but a few others dodged his attack and there was new rumbling in the legion.

'Together, demons, we can win this!' the hybrid shouted, now far enough away from William to be able to dodge his bolts but going from group to group, whispering sly encouragement to the others.

Claire and Raphael were spent. They knew they would have had a small chance of escape if only they had the energy to move. Both realised that all they had done was to delay their demise. There was small satisfaction knowing that the evil-eyed demon would be destroyed by his own kind. The chaos was all around them. Wherever they looked, they saw demons, intent on destroying William, and while they were awake, they were unable to block out his agonising screams.

'Try to stay awake, my love.'

'Why, Raphael, what's the point?' Claire decided she would prefer to be out of it when the time came, and her eyes flickered. She knew she was losing the fight.

Raphael kissed her forehead, enveloped her in a hug, and took one last look at his beautiful angel before closing his eyes.

Neither felt the invisible force pulling them slowly upwards, away from the battling monsters.

Epilogue

It was the last working Friday before Christmas, and Tony and Jim were on a video call with the Director and Violet before taking a week off to be with their families over the holiday. This year, that would include Dee and Daniel. They were, however, on call for most of the break except for Christmas Day and Boxing Day when Ryan and Janine took a turn.

'How's Daniel?' the Director asked.

Jim explained that he was well and had settled in to his new life in England. 'I can't say that he's looking forward to starting a new school in the new year, and he wasn't keen on the name change, but understands it was a necessity and part of the programme to protect him.'

'I may have a better solution to the school issue,' the Director said, 'but first, how's Eva, Tony?'

'She's fine thanks. No major incidents since the hornet attack, people and animals still seem to be drawn to her and Dee's a fantastic asset to her protection team.'

'Asset?'

'That's right. She's perfect for the job.'

Jim sniggered and his brother gave him a dirty look.

'Any information from your sister about her guards on the other side?' Violet asked.

'No,' the twins said together.

Jim continued, 'We haven't heard from Claire in a while, since before Ryan and I went to the States, in fact. From what Daniel can see, we know that there are always three guardians with Eva. It seems that one is with her most of the time and we assume that's Dee's brother, but the others change from time to time.'

'We've tried talking to Claire a number of times,' Tony added, 'but she hasn't shown up. It's a concern, but it's happened before and there's nothing we can do about it. I hope this isn't…' He stopped, and Jim squeezed his brother's shoulder, to comfort himself as much as Tony. When they didn't hear from their sister in a while there was always a worry that she'd gone for good, and if that was the case it would be like going through the grieving process all over again. Neither dared think what that would be like.

'I'm sorry,' Violet said. 'But at least Eva's protected which is some consolation.'

'Violet's right and, changing the subject, I have news about a new course in the New Year that I'd like you two to lead,' The Director said.

About to tell him he wouldn't be available, Violet must have read Tony's mind. 'Just hear him out first before saying anything,' she said.

'Okay.'

'For a while now, it's occurred to me that we're not utilising all human resources that could be available to us. Daniel's abilities and Eva's gifts, whatever they may be, have made me realise that we could induct and train Sunnies from a young age, in a boarding school environment.'

'That sounds like it would come with *so* many pitfalls,' Jim said. 'What would we tell the parents or guardians? And how would we convince them to let their children leave home at such a young age? Wouldn't it be too dangerous for the youngsters?'

'There's a disused wing, not far from the training centre in Brecon,' Violet responded, 'with lots of land. The Ministry of Defence haven't maintained it due to budget cuts and have agreed to sell the land and the building to Sir Paul, with some conditions, of course. He's already got his architects to draw up plans and estimate costs. As far as the parents are concerned, their children would be educated as part of the national curriculum, but their individual gifts, talents, or skills would be honed as part of the extracurricular activities. We wouldn't take anyone younger than eleven – except, maybe, for Eva but we can discuss that when she's older. These special children, potentially junior Sunnies, would be specially selected from all over the world and offered scholarships at the school. We estimate the building will be ready for use by the end of the summer, and you may wish to home-school Daniel until then, if you think he'd prefer that?'

'It sounds good to me and I'm in,' Jim said, 'as long as we can all move down during term time.'

'That's the plan,' the Director said. 'Tony?'

Tony took a few seconds to consider before responding. 'I'd move down with Dee and Eva, but what about Mum? She'd miss Eva so much if–'

'Marion's already told me that she wants to see Eva as much as she can, so I think she would want to move down with you all. Basil would need to base himself in or near Brecon for a while anyway – he'd need to carry out extensive assessment of the recruits so there's a real need for him to be there.'

'I don't think Mum will be happy about moving again,' Tony said, with a laugh.

The Director knew that he had him if his mother's reaction was Tony's main concern.

'Think about it over the break but let me know your response by the New Year,' he said, allowing Tony to think he was in charge of his own destiny.

'Will do, and we'll talk to Mum and Basil about it, too–and the girls, of course.'

They all wished each other the compliments of the season and finished the call. The twins looked at each other. 'I think I'm in,' Tony said, 'but let's see what the others say.'

They agreed to get Christmas over and done with and to discuss it during the weird time that fell after Christmas Day, but before the New Year.

When they re-joined the others, there was a discussion about whether to go for the long walk towards the common, or the short one to the park. The park won out and now the small group were all wrapped up and walking around the familiar lake in the park. It was crisp, dry and sunny, but cold – a perfect winter's day. Daniel was the only one wearing sunglasses; the light from Eva was so bright that from the first time he saw her, he knew couldn't be in her company without special eye protection.

She was out of her pushchair. He held one of her hands and Marion held the other. Spike trotted alongside Daniel. Eva stopped and looked adoringly at Daniel, giving him a big smile. The boy blew a raspberry which sent Eva into fits of giggles. When she stopped laughing, she looked first at her grandmother and then at Basil before letting go of Daniel's hand and turning around. Her little face was full of concentration and it seemed as if she was counting them off, or checking who was there, as she looked at her father and Dee, then Jim and Fiona who were behind them. Eva then looked towards the lake where a number of ducks had been following the group from way back before the lake. The birds had entered the water as soon as the lake came into sight and now swam alongside them.

'Ucks,' Eva said, and laughed again as the birds quacked a response.

Finally, Eva looked upwards and smiled. Daniel dropped back until he was alongside Tony and Dee. 'I can see three different colours up above,' he said quietly. 'The blue one that's almost always there, one orange and a yellow. The blue one's hovering between you and Eva, Dee, and the other two are around Eva.'

'Thanks, Daniel,' Dee said.

'You're welcome,' he replied. Satisfied that he'd done his job by passing them the information,

212

Tony and Dee watched as he headed back towards Marion, Basil and Eva.

'I guess the blue one must be Trevor then?' Dee said.

'I guess you're right,' Tony replied, lifting her hand and linking it through his arm.

Behind them, Fiona gave Jim a knowing look. 'Do you think they've…?'

'I've no idea,' said Jim, 'and I don't plan on asking him any time soon.'

'I suppose with the twin thing you'll know without having to ask, anyway,' she said, and elbowed him in the waist, before adding, 'Nudge, nudge.'

'I flaming hope not!' Jim said, laughing. He tickled his wife for a few seconds, raising gales of laughter from Fiona.

Tony looked around and smiled indulgently. When he turned back, Dee put her head on his shoulder, looked up at him, and whispered, 'This will give them something to talk about.' They both laughed.

'Look! Look at them now!' whispered Fiona.

'For Pete's sake woman, leave them alone!'

Fiona and Jim both chuckled, and the entire group carried on with their winter's walk.

Acknowledgements

Thanks to my husband Allan, to my awesome editor Jill Turner, and to Jessica Bell for another fantastic cover. Thanks also to all of my friends for their support, especially Julie, Trudy, Su, Tina, Craig, Libby, Debbie, Helen, and Jo.

Thank you for purchasing this book. If you have time to leave a short review so that other readers can find my books, I'd be extremely grateful.

Another Author's Note

This may be the last of my Afterlife books for a while, but then again, it may not! If you enjoyed this series you may be interested in my other books:

Unlikely Soldiers Book 1 (Civvy to Squaddie)
Unlikely Soldiers Book 2 (Secrets and Lies)
Unlikely Soldiers Book 3 (Friends and Revenge)
Unlikely Soldiers Book 4 (Murder and Mayhem)

Court Out (A Netball Girls' Drama)

Zak, My Boy Wonder (non-fiction)

The Island Dog Squad Book 1 (Sandy's Story)
FREE AT THIS LINK
https://dl.bookfunnel.com/wdh6nl8p08
The Island Dog Squad Book 2 (Another Secret Mission
The Island Dog Squad Book 3 (People Problems)

And for children:

Jason the Penguin (He's Different)
Jason the Penguin (He Learns to Swim)

Reindeer Dreams

Further information is on my website https://debmcewansbooksandblogs.com or you can connect with me on Facebook:
https://www.facebook.com/DebMcEwansbooksandblogs/?ref=bookmarks

About the Author

Following a career of over thirty years in the British Army, Deb and her husband moved to Cyprus to become weather refugees.

She's written children's books about Jason the penguin and Barry the reindeer and young adult/adult books about dogs, soldiers, and netball players, as well as a non-fiction book about a boy born to be different. Her most popular books are the supernatural suspense Afterlife series.

Although you've read the series, you may not know that it was inspired by ants. Deb was in the garden contemplating whether to squash an irritating ant or to let it live and wondered whether anyone *up there* decides the same about us and thus the series was born. Book 6, 'Beyond Sunnyfields' is currently in the planning stage.

The first book in the Unlikely Soldiers series is set in nineteen-seventies Britain. The second covers the early eighties and includes the Falklands War, service in

Northern Ireland and (the former) West Germany. 'Friends and Revenge' is the third in the series and takes a sinister turn of events. 'Murder and Mayhem' is the final book of the series and takes our heroine from the former West Germany, to London and to an action-packed Hong Kong.

'Court Out (A Netball Girls' Drama)' is a standalone novel. Using netball as an escape from her miserable home life, Marsha Lawson is desperate to keep the past buried and to forge a brighter future. But she's not the only one with secrets. When two players want revenge, a tsunami of emotions is released at a tournament, leaving destruction in its wake. As the wave starts spreading throughout the team, can Marsha and the others escape its deadly grasp, or will their emotional baggage pull them under, with devastating consequences for their families and team-mates?

'Zak, My Boy Wonder', is a non-fiction book co-written with Zak's Mum, Joanne Lythgoe. Deb met Jo and her children when she moved to Cyprus with Allan in 2013. Jo shared her story over a drink one night and Deb was astounded, finding it hard to believe that a family could be treated with such cruelty, indifference and a complete lack of compassion and empathy. This sounded like a tale from Victorian times and not the twenty-first century. When Deb suggested she share her story, Jo said she was too busy looking after both children – especially Zak who still needed a number of surgeries – and didn't have the emotional or physical energy required to dig up the past. Almost fourteen years later, Jo felt ready to share this harrowing but inspirational tale of a woman and her family who refused to give up and were determined not to let the judgemental, nasty, small-minded people grind them down.

'The Island Dog Squad' is a series of novellas inspired by the rescue dog Deb and Allan adopted in

2018. The real Sandy is a sensitive soul, not quite like her fictional namesake, and the other characters are based on Sandy's real-life mates.

Deb loves spending time with her husband Allan and rescue dog Sandy. She also loves writing, keeping fit, and socialising, and does her best to avoid housework.

Printed in Great Britain
by Amazon